Fireworks, Forensics, and Felonies

Book 7 in
The New Orleans Go Cup Chronicles

Colleen Mooney

Dedication

In memory of my father,
Thomas Joseph Mooney,
who shared his love of
fireworks and boating with me!

FIREWORKS, FORENSICS & FELONIES
The New Orleans Go Cup Chronicles series
Book Seven
Copyright © 2019, Colleen Mooney all Editions & Formats
Print Edition

Digital
13 digit ISBN: 978 1-7337387-2-9
10 digit ISBN: 1-7337387-2-X

Paperback
13 digit ISBN: 978 1 7337387-3-6
10 digit ISBN: 1-7337387-3-8

Chapter One

4th of July

THE SMELL OF gunpowder is an aphrodisiac to me. That's why I've always loved fireworks. I love setting them off, not just watching. I love the smell that lingers in the air. My dad taught me how to light a cherry bomb when I was three years old. He struck a match, handed it to me and while he held the cherry bomb, he said, "C'mon, you light it. I'll throw it. It's gonna be loud."

What I remember most was the smell that hung in the air after the boom. From that first blast that went off fifteen feet from the porch we were standing on, I've been crazy for fireworks. Every year I helped my dad set up and light the fireworks for New Year's, the 4th of July, when the Saints won the Super Bowl...any reason we needed additional celebration power over the customary bottle of champagne. Sometimes, Dante from next door helped us light them. I never missed a firework display, especially if I could be involved in lighting them.

My name is Brandy Alexander. I grew up next door to five boys. I learned early on not to let them know I was afraid of something, or those boys would have tortured me to death with it. Fireworks were different. I wasn't afraid of them, I loved them.

When I told Jiff this, he arranged to take his sailboat out on Lake Pontchartrain for the Fourth of July fireworks display and be downwind so we'd catch the aromatic aftermath. The thought of smelling an entire barge of explosives was something I was not going to say no to.

I've been dating Jiff Heinkel for the last year. We met at a Mardi Gras parade where he kissed me in exchange for a paper flower. Then, he asked me to meet him at the end of the parade and it was all over, except the shouting. Shouting and tears, lots of tears…loud, sobbing tears, really from Dante's mom. Dante is one of the five boys who lived next door to me growing up. Both sets of parents expected us to marry one day. Miss Ruth wanted us to marry because she loved me to death and wanted to see her son happy. My mother because she wanted me out of the house, the sooner, the better. Problem: Dante was not on the same page as our parents.

Now, Dante is with the New Orleans Police Department, Captain of the Homicide Division. It might have been the gunpowder from his weapons we used at the shooting range that kept me interested in him since he never did anything to indicate he wanted to move our future forward…together…until I met Jiff. Since then, he's been proclaiming his undying love. Dante's even gone so far as to welcome my help in his "ongoing investigations", something he was all too quick to run me off from in the past.

"Can I get you another glass of champagne?" Jiff asked. We were anchored out in Lake Pontchartrain on Jiff's sailboat listening to the waves gently kissing the side of the boat. It was the perfect night with a good breeze that made the sail here very enjoyable. Jiff's sailboat had a generator, air conditioning, and a generous bunk in the stateroom. It was a very comfortable yacht to spend the night on or take out to Ship Island in the Gulf and anchor for the weekend. Tonight, we could leave the hatches open and fall asleep to the sound of waves slapping at the hull, gently rocking us into a peaceful slumber.

"Yes, please," I said handing him my glass. "I hope we're in a good spot to get a whiff once the fireworks start." I stuck my nose up pretending I was sniffing the air to pick up the gunpowder smell like my Meaux does when I'm cooking in the kitchen. Meaux liked fireworks too. He was the only dog I ever had that didn't run and hide when they were exploding. Of course, Meaux just wanted to be wherever I was, regardless if he was afraid of loud noise or not.

"You'll smell it once it starts. I made sure we're downwind from the barge." He looked around over the water accessing our position. "If it blows much stronger, I don't know if Ian can still light them," he said kissing my forehead. "I would never lure you out here under the pretense of seeing fireworks or smelling gunpowder and then not deliver. You would never speak to me again. I'm hoping the giant show you are going to smell will put you in a very grateful mood."

"I'm already in a very grateful mood," I said putting my arms around him. "How do you know the guy who's putting on this extravaganza?"

"Ian and I went to Jesuit together. We worked on a science project in our senior year that involved blowing stuff up. He's a smart dude," Jiff answered. "Now, he works for the EPA. He's made a name for himself in the industry. Before you ask, fireworks have always been his thing. The City of New Orleans contracted him to set up this display in conjunction with the fireworks going off in Kenner, Slidell, and downtown on the Mississippi River."

"Ian works for the EPA, then explodes stuff into the air," I said. "Sounds like a dichotomy."

"Well, life is full of contradictions, isn't it?" Jiff said. "He also said he had something he wanted to run by me. He alluded to a discovery and wants my opinion on how to proceed. I thought we'd sail back to the harbor and go over to Ian's house in the morning and give them a hand getting ready for their barbecue. Their home is close to the marina. His wife's name is Sophie. You'll love her."

"Do you know what he wants to talk to you about?" I asked.

"No, but he sounded bothered by something and our schedules didn't allow us to meet until after the holiday weekend. He invited us to his house tomorrow for his 4th of July barbecue because he wants to meet you. They have a three-story, white stucco house—Miami Vice style—on Lakeshore Drive, just the other side of the levee, over there," he said and pointed to a large home we could only see the top floor and roof of sitting behind the grassy flood protection.

Jiff planned for us to spend the night on his sailboat. It was a big, roomy, and easy to handle forty-foot Beneteau with a master cabin that housed a queen size bed, not a bunk, a bed. All the winches were hydraulic so there was little to no cranking to hoist a sail, unless you just wanted to. You could just press a button. Jiff knew how to live.

I had asked Suzanne, my roommate, to dog sit my Meaux and Jiff's Isabella so we didn't have to go home to walk and feed our dogs. Jiff prepared a dinner of steaks and vegetables which he cooked on the grill attached to a stern guard rail. After dinner, we sat in the cockpit sipping champagne while we waited for the fireworks to start.

"The wind is starting to pick up," Jiff said. "This is a great night for sailing, but I hope this breeze doesn't give Ian problems with lighting his display or make it unsafe."

We had dropped the anchor just off the seawall near the New Orleans Lakefront airport. This way, we'd have a short sail back to the harbor, dock, and make the short drive to Ian and Sophie's home in the morning. Jiff advised he had planned a late breakfast for us to allow Ian and Sophie time to recover from tonight and get ready for their barbecue tomorrow afternoon. I was looking forward to a relaxing weekend with my guy and meeting his friends.

The night was clear, not a cloud in the sky. There was a good chance we would see the other displays set to go off across town on the Mississippi River next to the French Quarter and maybe the one in Kenner. They were all scheduled to start at 9:00 p.m.. The fireworks near the French Quarter started. We could see them and heard the soft pops and cracks in the distance. We moved to sit on the bow of the boat looking up in awe of the cracking, fiery display over our heads. Multiple bursts popped and lit up the sky. Ian's barge was scheduled to go off at the same time, but he was late. Once both displays were going, we'd be under a twinkling, dancing blanket of light.

"Ian outdid himself on the fireworks," Jiff said looking up after a particularly thunderous explosion in the direction across town.

"Yes, that last one was really loud," I said. "I felt the vibration all the way over here."

"Ian's company is Up in Smoke Fireworks. Wait until the end. He likes a grand finale," Jiff said and kissed my hand he was holding.

"I don't think that's part of the big ending," I said nodding toward a blaze on the other side of the levee, along Lakeshore Drive. "That last boom sounded like it came from there."

As we watched the smoke billowing under the lights cast by the fireworks display, Jiff stood up, never taking his eyes off the burning house and said, "That's Ian's house."

I jumped up with him. We stood watching the flames lick higher into the night sky. The smoke just got thicker and thicker. It started to drift over the sea wall across the water, making it hard to see Ian's barge in the distance. We watched as the wind started to pick up and feed the fire. It gained strength sending flames soaring into the night sky. Billowing black smoke shrouded the house creating intermittent views of the blaze.

Then, a giant second boom came. It was Ian's barge exploding.

Chapter Two

4th of July

AFTER THE EXPLOSION on the barge, Jiff and I moved into high gear. If nothing else told me Jiff was the right guy for me, the way we worked in crisis mode should have. However, for my entire life up until I met Jiff a year ago, I thought Dante was right for me. There was always a tiny, little, something that danced on my nerves whenever I thought of Dante. I started to doubt my own judgment when it came to the men in my life and which one was the right one for me. My dad always said 'some habits are hard to break,' suggesting Dante was a habit.

Jiff and I were in sync with each other's movements. If he reached for something, and I was closer, I handed it to him. He didn't have to ask. He did the same for me. If he worked the winch to raise a sail, I tailed it for him. We made a great team. I grew up on boats living in New Orleans. My dad always had one type of boat or another, and he taught me a love and respect for all things marine. My mother never learned to swim. She was terrified of the water. Boating was dad's great escape from my mother and he took me with him. It seems swimming and walking happened simultaneously for me. Dad also taught me to sail and snorkel at an early age.

"I'll get the anchor," Jiff said.

Since we had set anchor the wind gauge now showed it was blowing fifteen miles per hour, but also indicated a twenty-five mile per hour puff. The waves slapped the side of the boat and pushed it to a right angle from where we originally dropped the anchor.

"I'll start the engine," I said. We went about our tasks with the precision of a military maneuver.

"You'll have to put it in gear so I can winch up the anchor. The wind's blowing too hard for me to do it without an assist," Jiff yelled to me.

The anchor took longer to pull up with the wind not cooperating. I put the engine in neutral while he secured it in the anchor well. I went below to put in a Mayday call to the Coast Guard. While I was on radio with the Coast Guard telling them what we saw and the approximate location of the barge, Jiff came back to the cockpit and put the sailboat in gear, motoring over to the explosion. Every second counts in a rescue and we were both quiet in our thoughts wondering if we could get there in time to help.

The voice on the other end of the Coast Guard call advised me that they were out on another Mayday call with two more urgent calls pending. With the winds increasing it would likely be much later tonight before they would start a search and that depended on the weather not getting worse. Lake Pontchartrain on average had a depth of only fifteen feet so the wind was making for difficult conditions kicking up whitecaps in the size of two-foot waves.

I started to see debris floating down from the sky and landing all around us in the lake. It was hard to keep steady on my feet motoring over the waves. I needed one hand to hold onto something at all times. Jiff was holding onto the wheel. I kept my eyes peeled to the surface to see if I could spot anyone needing help. There wasn't much left of the barge. It had been blown in half and one end of each piece was at a forty-five-degree angle in the water.

Plastic, paper, remnants that made up the fireworks, were blowing down from the sky all around the barge as we approached. It made it hard to spot a person in the water if he or she was struggling or was unresponsive. Some of this debris could have landed on top of Ian. We searched for what felt like hours. We found no one.

"There's nothing left on that barge," I said as the wind pushed us about with the engine running at full power. "Where is the boat or tug that ferried it and Ian out here? How was Ian supposed to get back?"

"Maybe he planned to radio for a pick up," Jiff said, his eyes never leaving the water's surface. "Maybe they moved the tug for safety reasons with all the explosives out here. If a spark ignited the fuel on a boat, it would have gone up too." He finally looked at me and asked, "Why are you asking that?"

"It just seems that if safety was the concern, why leave someone out here alone in case of an accident? It seems there should have at least been a fire boat nearby in case this or something happened. How was he supposed to get help?"

"I don't know. Ian always said it was safe, and even so, he took every precaution," he said. "But, you're right, there should have been a fire boat or Ian's party boat waiting for him."

"We were busy looking at the house fire when that explosion happened. Didn't it sound like one big boom? I would have guessed that fireworks would have started going off one at a time, just in rapid succession, don't you think?"

"I don't know. That's something to ask whoever comes out to investigate," Jiff said.

Jiff and I searched for over an hour until the wind picked up even more. We didn't have as much control to try to stay out under power. Putting the sails up seemed counterproductive to searching. It seemed doubtful we would find Ian alive, if at all. We motored back in silence, constantly fighting the wind until we reached the harbor. We docked the boat in the slip and drove to Ian and Sophie's home to see if there was anything we could do. Their house was a five-minute drive from the marina.

Lakeshore Drive is a prestigious road along Lake Pontchartrain with the city's best and most beautiful homes showcased there. From what I could see, the flames had taken over Ian and Sophie's entire home and were shooting high into the air through the roof.

We made our way as close as we could manage to the upwind perimeter already set by the firefighters working the scene. The fire was in full force and angrily fighting attempts to be smothered. The smell of burning wood permeated the air. Cracking sounds of the fire breaking the frame of the house along with the sound of the inside collapsing was heartbreaking. The blaze was roaring when we arrived and the wind had picked up even more in the fifteen minutes since we left the harbor and drove here. Firefighters were struggling to get the blaze under control. Two more Fire Department trucks were pulling up when we arrived. Every imaginable vehicle from the Arson Team and Police Department were at the scene or arriving.

"Well, Miss Alexander. How did this happen?" a

voice I recognized was calling my name. It was Detective Taylor who asked standing near an unmarked police car circling his Mont Blanc pen in the air over his notebook like he was stirring coffee. He stood amid the entire New Orleans Police and Fire Departments dashing about with great determination without as much as a glance in our direction. Only Detective Taylor was staring at me.

"We, well I," Detective Taylor said, "arrived at this crime scene before you did. You did beat Captain Deedler here. Some traditions should remain unbroken. He'll be happy to hear it." Detective Taylor smiled at me and added, "Here he comes now. You can tell him yourself."

Dante stopped at the Fire Chief's car to speak with him. I wasn't sure if he had spotted me yet.

Detective Taylor worked for Dante, and on top of all that, I usually showed up at their crime scenes before they, or any of the police, did. Taylor was right, this was a first. Detective Travis Taylor stood out from the regular homicide detectives in the unit. He was a tall, attractive, fit transferee from New York City's finest. His steely, black eyes could make you very uncomfortable when he locked his gaze on you. He only wore custom suits and thin-soled Italian loafers. Everything he owned or used had a recognizable logo on it. He flirted with me as long as there was no chance of Dante hearing him. I had no interest in encouraging his attention. My life with the NOPD was complicated enough. Jiff and I had fallen into a wonderful, comfortable stride that I felt would only improve as we moved through life together.

When Dante walked up to Taylor, he spotted me standing with Jiff. He nodded an acknowledgement and I heard him ask Detective Taylor, "Whatcha got?"

Taylor said, nodding in our direction, "They know the people who live here. They walked up right after me. I'm waiting on the Fire Chief to give me an update."

"Brandy. Counselor," Dante said by way of hello as he and Taylor walked over to us. "How do you know the people who live in this house?"

"I didn't know them. They are friends of Jiff's," I said. "We were supposed to come to a barbecue here tomorrow."

"So, what are you doing here now?" Dante asked looking back and forth from me to Jiff.

Jiff said, "We were out on my sailboat waiting for the fireworks on the lake to start when we heard this explosion first. While we watched these flames soar into the air, we then heard the barge explode. We motored over to see if we could help with any recovery. When we didn't find anyone, we came here."

I noticed Detective Taylor ever so slightly raised his eyebrows when he heard Jiff mention we were on his sailboat. He was looking at me without blinking.

"Yes, Detective Hanky's contacting the Coast Guard about the barge explosion," Dante said.

"How do you know the victim, or should I say, victims? The person who owns this house and the one on the barge?" Detective Taylor asked. He never stopped looking at me while his pen was poised in midair ready to write down any vital information or facts we might relay.

"I've known Ian since high school. We were in law school together. Ian Saucier. He worked for the EPA. He was on that barge that exploded in the lake earlier. This is his house. His wife...his wife Sophie... might still be inside," Jiff said to Dante and Taylor.

"Both killed on the same night." Taylor said more to himself now tapping his pen on his leather bound notepad which I just noticed has his initials embossed on it. He turned to Dante and said, "Firemen couldn't get inside when they arrived. A neighbor I interviewed said he thought he saw someone go in the side door right before the explosion, but he didn't get a good look so he couldn't tell who it was. The firemen are just trying to put it out at this point. I'll call you and let you know what they find."

Dante left and nodded his goodbye to me. He more or less ignored Jiff, but Jiff didn't seem to notice. He was too intent on watching Sophie and Ian's house burn.

"I'll let you know if they find your friend in there. I

hope she got out or wasn't in there to begin with. Could she be at a friend's house?" Detective Taylor asked me after Dante had left.

"I hope so," I said. "Both explosions, the house and the firework barge, happened within seconds of each other. I was looking at the barge when the house exploded and looking at the house when the barge exploded. I wasn't looking directly at either one when it happened."

Taylor just looked at me, and I knew what he was thinking. It crossed my mind as well... it was a mighty big coincidence if you believed in coincidences. I didn't and I knew a homicide detective didn't either. Jiff walked off to speak to one of the firemen.

"Do you think they are connected?" Taylor asked me.

"I don't see how they could not be connected," I said keeping an eye on Jiff to see when he headed back to us. "The barge explosion seemed too big for fireworks alone. You know how sound travels over water," I said to Taylor.

"You said you didn't see it happen. What do you mean?" Taylor asked me. "Weren't you out there on your boyfriend's sailboat to watch it?"

"I've been around fireworks all my life, and that boom was all at one time, and very, very loud. Too loud for just fireworks. I don't care how big they were supposed to be, that boom sounded like it could take down a building. I don't understand why they exploded all at one time instead of incrementally. If they were ignited all at the same time—even accidentally—they still would not have gone off all at the same time, right?" I said.

"Fireworks are outta my league. I'll have to get the arson guys to look into it," he said.

Jiff's friend, the guy on the fireworks' barge, wanted to talk to him about something tomorrow after the picnic. If we find out what that might be, I'll let you know." I turned to walk over and stand next to Jiff.

Taylor just nodded. Detective Travis Taylor had been an early believer that I actually had something to offer in solving a crime when I had the misfortune to be at the scene when it happened. Dante was just coming around to that belief, but much more slowly— at glacial speed. I worked for a major telecom company in their fraud department. My uncanny ability to find inconsistencies in data entries serves my clients well, but it's particularly helpful in everyday situations, or in this case, crime scenes. I see, feel or sense, what is off or doesn't fit. It's not an exact science. It can be anything from data entries to how someone looks when he or she answers a question. The only way I can explain it is that I notice the insignificant that doesn't fit the pattern.

A man about our age approached Jiff. They obvi- ously knew each other from the bro-hug they exchanged. It looked like Jiff was telling this man about the barge and pointing out to the lake. As I walked up to them, Jiff said by way of introduction, "This is Phillip."

"Hi, I'm Brandy."

"Sorry to meet you like this. I was supposed to meet Angie here tonight to watch the fireworks with Sophie on the levee," Phillip said as he ran both hands through his hair and landed them with fingers intertwined on top of his head. He looked terribly distraught.

"Why didn't you go with Ian to help him on the barge tonight?" Jiff asked him. "Isn't this usually a big display on the 4th?"

"Yes, it is our biggest. Angie's brother, Freddie, went with Ian tonight. I had to make the delivery for the other big display we have at the riverfront, so Ian took Freddie to help him."

"So you don't know what happened to them?" Jiff asked him.

"No, what?" he asked looking back and forth from my face to Jiff's.

After Jiff told him, Phillip needed to sit down. We walked him over to sit on the back bumper of Jiff's Mercedes.

"I need to call Angie and tell her to try to find Freddie. He was supposed to be going with Ian tonight to help him," he said and pulled out his cell phone. Phillip just sat there looking at his phone as if he didn't know what to do with it. When he finally pushed the buttons to call his wife, we heard him tell her he would stay here until she came to get him.

There was nothing else we could do here at the fire, so we decided to go back to the boat for the night as originally planned. We rode in silence back to the marina. As we walked down the pier, I said, "I'm sorry for the loss of your friends." I didn't want to tell him that I heard Taylor tell Dante a neighbor thought they saw a man go inside the house right before the explosion. It could be Ian went back home for something and maybe he was in the house also. It would be best to wait for an ID.

Jiff just nodded and put his arm around my neck as we made our way back to the slip where his boat was docked.

Jiff and I sat in the cockpit with a glass of wine. Both of us were thunderstruck by what had happened, but he was way more distracted than I was. He knew them both. I hadn't met them yet.

It was late now, almost 2:00 am when we heard the Coast Guard vessel and the Fire Boat motoring back into the harbor towing a Hatteras that obviously couldn't get back under their own power.

"It seems like a very big coincidence that they both met with their end at the same time, don't you think?" I asked.

"That was no coincidence. Now I wish I knew what he wanted to talk to me about," he said.

Chapter Three

Monday am @ work

IAN'S BODY WAS not recovered and the search was called off the next day, Friday. Only one tennis shoe, believed to be his, was found floating in the debris. I sat in my office on Monday morning unable to stop thinking and rethinking about these 4th of July disasters involving Jiff's friends.

There was no positive DNA found in the immediate aftermath of the house fire. It was a five thousand square foot house, and the roof collapsed onto the second floor, causing it to collapse onto the first. If Sophie was on the first or second floor, her body could have been incinerated, burning in a superhot fire and then smoldering for hours before the firemen put it out and the arson team could investigate. The coroner would have to decide if there was enough DNA to establish identification from the cremated remains.

The house fire and the barge explosion were too much of a convenience or coincidence. The timing, the explosions happening almost at the same time, and involving the same people were all red flags. If we had any idea what Ian wanted to talk to Jiff about, maybe it would shed some light on what happened and why.

By lunchtime I had written down several questions and filled about three pages full of doodles. Sometimes doodling helps me think. Not today. I wanted to know the answers...now. I went out to grab a bite for lunch, and when I returned, I sat at my computer trying to concentrate on finding a client's fraudulent activity in his computer system when my cell phone rang. It was Jiff.

"Hey, how's it going?" I answered.

"I got something very interesting in this morning's mail," Jiff said. "Can I pick you up after work? I want you to see this and give me your thoughts."

"Sure. I'll probably be able to leave here about 5:30. I can walk over to your office and meet you."

Jiff worked in the law firm his grandfather established with his dad and brothers. It started as a family business that hired several other attorneys as they grew. Now, their offices took up two floors in One Canal Place. It was a prestigious address. While I had my own office, with a door, and a team of five that reported to me, my office was in an old telephone company central office that had been used back in the days of enormous switching equip.m.ent. The big equip.m.ent was gone and modular offices had sprung up in its place. Now, my department was the last remnants of the previous footprint. Not glamorous, nor prestigious, purely functional. The rest of the building was leased as downtown warehouse space, but I had a feeling that was going to change too. Rumor had it that the building was recently sold to an investor who planned to turn it all into condos. My office and team would likely be moved out of the high rent district or work out of our homes. Ugh.

"I'll pick you up. Let's go someplace private where we can talk," he said.

"What's this about?" I asked as my interest piqued.

"I'd rather show you. I want you to see it like I saw it, then give me your opinion," he said. Jiff always valued my input on things we worked on together. We had been thrown together on a couple of his investigations for clients and even on some I hadn't planned on being involved in.

"Okay, give me a buzz when you leave your building and I'll be downstairs waiting," I said.

"See you at 5:30," he said and hung up.

Trying to concentrate on anything work related now was out of the question. I decided to call my hairdresser and see if she had an opening to give me a trim. Jeffrey said she could squeeze me in if I could get there in five minutes. It was a short three-minute walk away from my office building to her salon on Poydras Street in One Shell Square. The building's original name of One Shell Square was changed when a bank bought it. It will always be One Shell Square to me and most New Orleanians. We are slow to change, if we change at all. New Orleanians are still calling the Crescent City Connection—the new name for the Mississippi River Bridge for well over fifteen years now—the Mississippi River Bridge. The Crescent City Connection sounds like a dating service. Whereas, calling it the Mississippi River Bridge lets you know exactly where it is, and that it is what gets you across that big muddy waterway that is treacherous to all ships or watercraft trying to navigate it.

Jeffrey's salon was on the first floor with a floor to ceiling view of the corner of Poydras and Carondelet Street from her chair by the window. The one chair opposite Jeffrey had the same view. This was a front row seat for watching all of New Orleans, from the well suited Captains of Industry to young girls baring more skin than was covered by their clothing, go by.

"Hey, dawlin'," Jeffrey greeted me with a hug and a kiss. She swept the hair on the floor and put the broom into the corner. "Hop in my chair. I haven't seen you in a while. What's up?"

"Just a trim. You know my definition of a trim. You cut off so little, you feel guilty charging me," I said smiling as we both nodded in agreement. I sat in her chair and she whipped a large black smock over the suit I was wearing, pinching the Velcro together snuggly around my neck. She had been my hairdresser for years and has heard this definition every time I have had an appointment.

Jeffrey was a fount of information which she gleaned from the business men and women executives who sat in her chair or passed through her shop. There were six other hairdressers in this salon and all the chairs faced the center with a mirror down the middle, so you could hear what other patrons were talking about unless they really lowered their voice. Then you had to lean forward a little and shush your stylist to eavesdrop on a juicy bit of gossip.

She started combing my hair with one hand and holding scissors in the other.

"I guess you heard about the big explosion on the lake yesterday. There was a fire at the couple's home almost at the exact same time. Jiff and I were out on his sailboat waiting for the fireworks to start when it happened."

"I heard it on the news," she said nodding. "I had a barbecue at my house for the 4th and my whole family came. My brother and Ant-knee was there. You remember Ant-knee? He has the company that cleans graffiti off walls, buildings, bridges, interstate signs, you name it."

Jeffrey and her entire family pronounced Anthony, a name with three syllables—Ant-knee, with only two syllables. This was a common mispronunciation in New Orleans since one of the most centrally located churches, St. Anthony, was also pronounced St. Ant-knee by the entire congregation.

"Oh yes, I remember Anthony? How is he?" I asked trying not to sound like I said his name correctly. Jeffrey never noticed.

"Good. He's good. I always tell him he'll have to will that company to someone. He's got a career opportunity with the graffiti in this city," she said smiling as she combed and snipped. "He can't clean it off fast enough before someone is adding more right behind him." Jeffrey always had a smile on her face. "Someone mentioned the fireworks explosion and Ant-knee said he was working in an abandoned building along Tchoupitoulas on July 3rd. There was some homeless guy in it that told him he saw boxes of dynamite in there. He told Ant-knee he just missed the guy who came and took three or four boxes. Ant-knee asked him how did he know they were dynamite and the guy said, 'It said DYNAMITE on the boxes. I can read. I'm homeless, not illiterate.'

"Why on earth would anyone pick that building to sleep in if it was filled with explosives—what if someone threw a cigarette in there?" I asked.

"Ant-knee asked the guy the same thing, but only got a shrug for an answer before the guy went back to sleep," Jeffrey answered. "What can you say? People are crazy everywhere, but here, they're usually drunk and crazy."

She was right. I needed to talk to that homeless guy camping out in that vacant building. I asked Jeffrey, "Can I talk to Anthony? Maybe he can give me the address of that building so I can see who owns it," I said. "Maybe that's who had dynamite stored there. The timing fits the explosion on the lake." I paused thinking—dynamite. Moved on the 3rd of July. Barge with fireworks explodes. "Do you think Anthony will talk to me?"

"Yes, he'll talk to you. Be patient. He's not quick to return calls but he'll get around to it. I'll text you his phone number, but be careful. You might find out more than you want to know. Maybe you should let the police handle it." Jeffery said.

"Sure. I'll just pass along the info to the lead detective," I said.

"That's not Dante, is it? I thought you two were a thing of the past," she said.

"No-o-o-o, it's not Dante. I'm not with him anymore, but it does seem like I see more of him now than I did when we dated," I said.

"Why is that?" Jeffrey asked, her scissors stopped snipping in mid-air.

"When we were dating, he was never around. He always had to leave to run to a crime scene. Now that we're not dating, it seems I bump into him every time I turn around," I said.

Jeffrey started trimming again. "Hmmm. Uh huh," Jeffrey said. Her nonchalant comments had a way of soliciting more information from you than any question could.

"I guess Dante and I will always be connected on some level. We've known each other our entire lives, and with Jiff's firm always representing someone who has been arrested for one thing or another, it stands to reason I'll run into him now and then," I said.

"Watch him. Don't let him mess up a good thing you've got with your new guy," Jeffrey said.

"No," I said closing my eyes and shaking my head until she grabbed it with both hands to keep it still so she would not butcher my trim. "Jiff values my input and help on his cases. That's more than Dante ever did."

"Dante sounds like he doesn't want to deal with the fact it's over between you," she said. "He's happy to keep running into you and hoping you've changed your mind."

"Funny you should say that. When I told him it

was over, he said, 'I'll wait for as long as it takes.'" I asked him, 'As long as it takes for what?' He must think this is a temporary thing."

"That's because men don't have the 'brace yourself for the end of a relationship gene," Jeffery said still snipping away at the ends of my hair. "They do have the 'why would any woman end a relationship with me' gene. If it's not their idea to end it, they can't fathom why you would."

"You're right," I said, trying not laugh and move my head.

After my trim I went straight to a coffee shop on Poydras about a block away from my office. I heard my cell phone ping with a new message. Jeffrey had sent me Anthony's number so I called him. When he didn't answer, I left a message. I imagined he was hanging over the side of a building, cleaning and painting over graffiti someone left ten stories up. It might be hours before he called me back so I took about twenty minutes to sit and drink a cup of coffee, wondering what Jiff had for me to read. With my obsessive compulsive self, I'd alternate between wondering what Jiff had to show me and what else Anthony might know that could help with the investigation. I needed a distraction from my distractions. I went back to work. Now, I had to wait until 5:30 p.m. for Jiff to pick me up to see what he wanted me to read.

Chapter Four

Monday p.m. after work

JIFF WAS PARKED and waiting for me when I walked out of my building at 5:30 p.m.. He wrapped his arms around me in a loving, tender embrace ending in a warm hello kiss. That man had a way of kissing me, like the first kiss we exchanged in the middle of a Mardi Gras parade, making me feel as if my clothes were melting off. In my ear, he said, "That fire and explosion made me realize how much I have to lose with you."

Wow. Jiff always said he knew we were made for each other and wanted to spend his life with me. This felt like he was hinting at moving the timeline up to make that happen.

"I'm not going anywhere anytime soon," I said trying to lighten the moment.

"Well, wherever you go, I'm going with you," he said engulfing me in another tender hug.

"So, where are we going?" I asked. "And, what is it

you want me to eyeball before we discuss it?"

Jiff opened the passenger door and handed me an envelope as I slid in the passenger seat of his Mercedes. I glanced at the envelope. Ian's name and address were in the upper left corner.

The letter was handwritten, neatly printed, then signed by Ian. It was dated and time stamped at 8:30 am on the 4th of July which fell on a Thursday. Today was Monday after the Thursday holiday. Lots of people took Friday off for a long weekend, so things like the mail were just getting back to normal.

I took the letter out of the already opened envelope. It read:

Jiff, if you're reading this and we didn't meet over the 4th, then something terrible has happened. Please talk to Esme Bourgeois—Sophie's sister. You should remember her. We all went to law school together. She's an attorney here in New Orleans practicing family law. She lives alone on Esplanade Avenue near the Fairgrounds. We wanted Esme to have a Power of Attorney for each of us and the business. I already gave her my POA in case anything ever happened to me so Sophie would have someone to help her make decisions. Relax. My login and passwords are at the end of this letter. Esme is a trusted member of our family. Also know I trust Phillip Wilson like I trust you.

Believe whatever he tells you.

There was the address and phone number at the end of the note for Esme. It was signed, Ian Saucier.

Attached to Ian's letter was a draft of a contract for a new business. Ian's notes were scribbled on it, *'Here are the main points I want it to cover in a contract. Please look it over and add Sophie as an equal partner with Phillip and I. I need you to put it in your legal lingo. If something should happen to me, have my share go directly to Sophie. The lab is ready to go, and Sophie has done a lot of work helping me get this off the ground. She's getting her license and accreditation to do the testing.'*

"Wow, this is a ton of info," I said. "It sounds like Ian had an inkling something was going to happen to him."

"There's something else," he said.

I looked at him and gave him the hand move of rolling forward to continue.

"An insurance adjuster called me today about a claim made on the million-dollar life insurance policy recently taken out on Ian Saucier and another one made on Sophie Saucier. Maybe we should locate Ian's computer and see if there's anything on it that might point to who could have done this," Jiff said. "Why else would he give me the login?"

"Doesn't it seem like he would have given Phillip, his partner, the logins, or maybe he just didn't get around to it yet. They did have this big 4th of July party planned," I said.

"I don't know. Have you heard from the police?" Jiff said.

"No, I haven't. How did Ian get to the barge that night?" I asked. "Someone must have ferried him out to it."

"Sophie and Ian have a boathouse at the marina. I think they have a party barge they keep docked there. He also belonged to the yacht club so let's start there. The Committee Boat might have planned to take him and pick him up from the barge," Jiff said. "Why are you asking that?"

"I'm wondering who saw him last, that's all," I said.

"Oh, right," Jiff answered. "I need to get my head in the game. I don't mind telling you the loss of these two friends at the same time has me rattled."

"We are assuming Sophie was in that fire. We don't know that yet," I said. "Taylor or Hanky might be willing to confirm that much, if not to us, then at least to Sophie's sister Esme. Then we can talk to her. How's that sound? I'll call and see if Hanky or Taylor will give us any info." When Jiff gave me a sideways look, I added, "You never know."

"Yeah. Sounds fine," Jiff said.

Detective Taylor picked up on the first ring. He was the far better option to ask for a favor than his partner, Detective Hanky. Hanky used to be Dante's partner and while we got off on the wrong foot, it all seemed to have worked itself out. She was, however, very loyal to Dante and, in all likelihood, would ask him if it was OK to give me the info. He would say no.

"Homicide. Taylor," he answered.

"Why, Detective Taylor, you're still at the office, hard at work," I said.

"Yes, Miss Alexander, just waiting to see if I could be of service to you. I know you're calling for something, so let me see if I can guess," he said.

"If you don't guess correctly, I'll still ask," I said.

"Well, to save us both time, I'm thinking it's about the fire. You want to know whether or not we found a body, and if it was identified. Am I close?"

"Yes!" I said. "Did you find a body and have you identified it?"

"Now why should I tell you?" he asked.

"Because you are a nice guy and you know if I find out something, I'm coming straight to you or your Captain to give you the info," I said in my nicest voice. "We know the family and they might tell us something they won't tell the police."

"Right. I was born at night, but it wasn't last night," he said.

"So let me talk to Dante," I said.

"So far, there were remains found in the fire, but

they have not been identified. Sadly, there was someone in that fire, but I can't tell you who," he said.

"Oh no…I was hoping she got out of there," I said, my heart sinking.

"Yeah, me too," Taylor said. "I'm sorry."

"Thanks. We are going to see the family to see if there's anything we can do. I'll let you know if they tell us anything useful," I said. "Now, transfer me to Dante, please."

"He's not in his office. I'll tell him to call you, and, Miss Alexander, you need to stay out…"

"Talk to you soon, bye," I cut him off and hung up. I noticed we weren't headed to either of our homes. "Where are you taking me?" I asked Jiff.

"To the yacht club to see if they can tell us how Ian got out to the barge," he said. "Half of the members are in the Coast Guard Auxiliary."

Monday p.m.

TOM, THE MANAGER of the yacht club was sitting in his office when Jiff and I entered the building. He had a floor to ceiling glass wall overlooking the entrance and rear exits to the lobby. It reminded me of a fish bowl. On Mondays the restaurant was closed. Tom started frantically waving at us to get our attention before we took the elevator up and found the dining room dark.

He got up from his desk and hurried to the lobby area, greeting us with a big smile saying, "Good evening, Mr. Heinkel," he said and then turned to me. "Miss," he said with a head nod. "Glad I stopped you if you were going up for dinner. The dining room is dark tonight but the bar is open tonight, until seven, only about another hour."

"Actually, we came here to see you," Jiff explained.

Tom looked back and forth to us, and it dawned on me he thought we might be coming to make some sort of party reservations. His manners were perfect and he waited to hear what it was we were wishing to discuss with him. He seemed like a likable guy used to solving issues at a private club where the members were demanding and expected a certain level of service that would impress the Queen of England. The bookcases were filled with large silver cups awarded to members of the yacht club who had won Olympic races, International and National Regattas up and down the East Coast, the Gulf of Mexico and in races to Cuba. Jiff had pointed out which trophies he had helped put in the case.

"Of course. Come into my office and have a seat," he said extending an arm to direct us into the fish bowl.

Once we had a seat, I noticed all of Tom's desk accessories were clear, very nice glass, or high end acrylic. His in/out trays, pen holder, picture frame with his wife's photo, stapler, paper clip dish—even his coffee mug—were all clear and transparent. Maybe Tom did like the fish bowl effect.

Jiff asked Tom if the racing committee boat was used the night of the fireworks display. Tom said no one used the committee boat on the 4th of July since there were no races sponsored by the club. No one used any of the vessels at the Yacht Club to ferry Ian to the barge.

"Are you sure?" I asked. "Could someone else have used the boat?"

"Yes, ma'am. I'm sure," he said smiling. "Only the Racing Committee Chairman has the keys to the committee boat and if it leaves the dock, he has to be on it. He was here on the grand lawn out behind the club all afternoon at the Fourth of July picnic with his family waiting to see the fireworks. I saw him there myself… all evening. After the explosion, he took his family to the dining room and ordered dinner to go. They left with their dinners about 9:30 p.m."

"Thanks, Tom," Jiff said and shook his hand as we left his office. "C'mon," he said to me. "There's a guy who lives on his sailboat in the marina, and he seems to know just about everything that goes on out here."

Jiff said we had to drive over to another section of the marina to access the pier where Jack docked his boat. His very large sailboat was in one of the big slips at the end of the pier facing a stretch of boathouses. Jiff explained that Jack's slip faced Ian's boathouse. We found Jack sitting in his cockpit topping off a tumbler from a fifth of Gosling's rum when we walked up. He invited us to board. We left our shoes on the pier and boarded his yacht.

From the very big cockpit we could see everything that happened in almost every boathouse where the lights were on. I'd have called Jack a bit of a voyeur.

"Like TV only better," Jack said to me when he noticed me looking around at the boathouses. "Have a seat. What can I get ya to drink? It's gotta be rum or rum. I don't have any mixers so it's straight up or with an ice cube."

"I'm good," I said. Jiff waved him off as good also.

"I'm sure there are some ladies swimsuits hanging on the back of the door in the head if you want to get out of your business suit and be more comfortable," he said. "You look hot."

"Okay, Jack, she's my girlfriend," Jiff gave him a playful push.

"Right, I just figured you might want to see more of her. I know I would," he said with a devilish smile and moved out of Jiff's reach. "Oh wait, I think I have some wine down there in the icebox. Wine? Would you like some? It's white."

"Sure," I said, and Jiff went along with me.

"Have a seat, relax and enjoy this little puff of wind we're having this evening. I'll be right back," Jack said and put both hands on either side of the hatch and lowered himself below without using the steps.

"Little puff of wind? It's blowing everything not securely strapped down off the boats and into the water. It feels like it's... puffing... thirty to forty knots," I said. "How long have you known Jack?"

"Everybody knows Jack. This yacht is a Hinckley. Probably the heaviest, and most expensive sailboat in this marina," he said. "Jack is a trust fund baby, but he works. He has a construction company that he calls Midnight Construction. He says if he works at night he doesn't have to bother getting permits from the city. He's a bit of a rebel."

I rolled my eyes and said "Ya think?" Just in the few minutes I had known Jack, I figured he was definitely a character. He was charming in a most unusual way. I liked him. His boat was older, but everything was pristine, from the lines coiled just so to the shine on the stainless winches, and the teak had a high polish finish on it. His yacht was the definition of ship shape even if Jack wasn't. He appeared to be three sheets to the wind, but maintaining a steady course on his feet.

"I don't remember how we met. I guess it was out here at the yacht club or a race, on somebody's boat somewhere," Jiff said. "If he likes you, he'll do anything for you."

"Including loaning you one of his ladies' swimwear off the hook below," I said.

Jack came up with two wine glasses filled to the brim with white wine. It was terrible, but we sipped it anyway. Jiff told him why we had come by after we were all seated with our drinks.

"This is a beauty of a sailboat," I said taking my glass.

"Take a look around. Go below and check her out," Jack said.

"I don't mind if I do. I like sailboats and I've never seen one like this," I said.

"You probably won't see another one like it in this harbor. She's a heavy cruiser and most boats out here are for racing. They are faster, lighter, quicker," he said. "But none are as comfortable for cruising or living aboard. If you change your mind about the swimsuits, help yourself."

I went below and it looked as orderly and clean as the deck. There was a huge master cabin with a queen size bunk and a full size refrigerator in the galley. I thought I most definitely could live on this. True to his word, Jack had four ladies' swimsuits hanging on a hook in the head off the master stateroom. All were brand new swimwear with the tags still on them. Jack was quite a well prepared character.

When I came back up I heard Jack telling Jiff what he saw the night of the 4th.

"I saw the party boat go out with Ian and some other guy. The other guy came back about thirty minutes later," he said.

"Did you see him leave?" I asked.

"I heard him leave," Jack said taking a large swallow of his drink. "I watched him do a piss poor job of tying up Ian's boat, so I decided to go over there and check to make sure it was secure with the weather kicking up. The guy was talking on his cell phone when he left the boat. I was walking over when I heard a motorcycle, a loud motorcycle, come screeching up behind the boathouses. By the time I got over to that side, I saw a motorcycle stop at the other end of the boathouses in front of Ian's. That guy hopped on the back and they rode off."

"Did you see the driver of the motorcycle?" I asked.

"No, because he had the good sense to have on a helmet. Unfortunately, it also had one of those dark windshields so I didn't see his face. He should have had on a jacket and long pants but instead, he had on a sleeveless T-shirt and both arms were covered in tats. He was riding a brand new bike," Jack said and took another gulp of his drink. "Looked like a Harley, low rider with the angel wing handlebars. You know, like you see biker gangs ride."

"Yes, I know what you mean," Jiff said, failing to sound non-judgmental.

Jack went down below to grab another bottle of Goslings since he emptied the one he had into his glass. I took the opportunity to dump most of my wine over the side. Jiff looked at me and said, "If I have to drink it, you should too."

"We should have had the rum with ice," I said.

We were both standing when Jack came back up on deck. Jiff thanked him for the drinks and info, adding he had to feed me before we both faded away into the air.

"Hey, come back Sunday and we'll take her out. We could go for a sail now. She loves this much wind. We won't even spill our drinks," Jack said.

"Sunday sounds good. I'll give you a call," Jiff said. "We'll bring wine."

"Mine was that bad, huh?" he said laughing.

I thanked Jack for the drink and said it was nice meeting him as we left his yacht. Once out of earshot, I asked Jiff, "Can he sail when he drinks like that?"

"He does everything like that. I've never seen Jack without a tumbler of rum, a full tumbler of rum, in his hand, but I've never seen him unable to handle himself or his boat."

As we walked back to his car, I suggested we grab something already made at one of the nearby food markets since most restaurants are closed on Mondays. We were close to his apartment, and one market in particular made a prepared crabmeat stuffed salmon roulade I loved and thought Jiff would like. All I had to do was heat it up for twenty minutes. We could get a side veggie to heat in the microwave also.

"My French is bad. Remind me what roulade is," he said.

"It's like a pinwheel of salmon rolled with crabmeat," I said.

"Oh right, that roulade," he said squeezing my hand.

"Let's pick up Isabella from your apartment and take her to play with Meaux," I said. "Suzanne usually puts him out before she leaves for work, but he's going to be hungry right about now," I said, checking my watch. It was going on 6:30 p.m. "I'll feed the two of them and then Isabella and Meaux can have a play date while we reread the letter, call Esme to see when we can speak to her, and sort out what we think we know from what we really know," I said.

"Good idea. My head's been messed up over this one," he said. "I'm glad I have you thinking clearly right now."

"I get it. All of you were friends," I said. "You're gonna like this roulade...pinwheel, I mean."

I FED THE dogs first. While I heated and prepared the food, Jiff set two places for us at the dining room table. While we ate, the two Schnauzers rough housed and body slammed each other until they wore themselves out. After our dinner, we sat on my sofa re-reading the letter with Meaux on one side of me, his head resting in my lap so he could read the letter along with me. I sat next to Jiff with Isabella on the other side of him.

"Sometimes Meaux sees things I miss," I joked to Jiff as I nodded toward Meaux looking at the page I was holding.

"They are a curious breed," he said. "Too bad they can't talk."

"I understand him plenty as it is," I said. "Meaux does not need words to let me know what he wants." I stopped and petted my dog a minute, then added, "I've read this letter so many times I have it memorized."

"Me too," he said.

"There's something between the lines here we're missing. Do you think Phillip could want to take over the business enough to want Ian gone? Is he that type?" I asked.

"Phillip? No," Jiff said. "He and Ian have been pals since they were kids. Let's call Esme and see if she'll meet with us. She might know more."

"How well do you know Esme?" I asked.

"Esme is Sophie's little sister. I met her when Ian

started dating Sophie in high school. Sophie always brought her along on outings or parties. She's a year younger than Sophie, and Ian tried to get me to take out Esme but I wasn't interested. Esme wasn't interested in me either. Actually, Phillip had a crush on Esme way back then."

"Interesting," I said. "She ever marry?"

"Not that I'm aware of. She was always very studious, more so than Phillip, Ian or I. She was two years behind us in high school but started law school with Phillip and Ian after they returned from their tour."

He made the call and Esme agreed to meet with us after work tomorrow. She was still reeling from the shock of losing her sister in the fire and Ian in the explosion. I could hear her speaking to Jiff over the phone from where I was sitting. I overheard Esme tell Jiff, "The police haven't ruled either death a homicide yet. They are waiting for the Arson Investigator to decide if they were accidental."

Chapter Five

JIFF AND ISABELLA spent the night. We were now at a phase of our relationship where we kept a change of clothes at each other's place. I suggested he leave Isabella with Meaux today and not bring her home. I liked it when Meaux and Isabella were company for each other. They got along great...no doggie arguments. Everything I've read tells me dogs just want to be around other dogs. Meaux, of course, wanted to be around me... and other dogs.

As soon as I woke up, I noticed Jiff's forehead was creased in worry lines even before he was fully awake. I fed the dogs before we left for work. Jiff gave me a ride since my car was still at the office from last night. It gave us a chance to plan what we might want to discuss with Esme.

"I wonder what Esme can tell us that might shed some light on this whole thing with Ian and Sophie," Jiff said.

"Maybe she knows more of what went on with the business. Esme must know Phillip and his wife," I said.

"Yes. She has known Phillip as long as she has known Ian. She probably spends time with the four of them socially through dinners or parties," Jiff said. "It could be why Ian wanted me to draft the contracts."

"Esme doesn't live far from me in Mid City. Let's meet at my house after work and we can go in one car if that's okay. I'll feed and play with the dogs until you get there."

Jiff nodded and the lines on his forehead didn't diminish even when he dropped me off and kissed me goodbye as I got out of his car.

THE WORRY LINES were still there when Jiff picked me up later that afternoon. When he drove up I was sitting on my front porch swing. I live in one side of a shotgun double. The landlord had put up a wrought iron hand railing dividing the porch, but he also added ceiling hooks on each side for his tenants to add a swing if we wanted. It was relaxing to sit out here, watch the neighborhood or wait for someone. Meaux often sat with me when I relaxed with a glass of wine.

Esme lived in a beautiful, lavender-colored two-story Victorian along Esplanade Avenue near the Fairgrounds. There was a complimenting color on the trim, windows and doors of a deep purple.

Jiff parked in the driveway alongside her home, which also led to a side garden, and I waited for Jiff to come open my door. He made a point of telling me to wait so he could walk around and open my car door for me. Chivalry might have been on life support with men in general, but it was alive and well with my guy. Nothing makes you feel more appreciated than a man with good manners who uses them to show he cherishes you. Even if you don't think it, everyone else will. I never wanted to take it for granted.

We made our way to the front porch that spread the entire width of the house. I stopped at the first step onto the porch. An inviting wicker swing and four wicker rockers were gently calling my name to spend a few minutes rocking or swinging the days' stress away. They also suggested doing it with a glass of wine in my hand. I'm sure Esme could hear Jazz Fest music from the Fairgrounds playing while sitting right here on her front porch. I would spend a lot of time on this porch if it were mine.

We headed to the shuttered front door. Esme lived in the main house and rented what looked like an apartment over the garage at the rear of the garden side of the property. I heard her open the door behind the storm shutters. I'm sure she could see who it was as she said, "Just a second while I unlock this side." When she opened the door, two Schnauzers ran out to greet us barking. I held my hand down and once I started to pet them, they were friends forever.

"You can't sneak up on me when I have Sparkler or Blast here. Blast is…" she stopped to rephrase, "was…Ian and Sophie's dog and Sparkler is mine. I guess Blast is mine now too." Then she gave Jiff a big hug. "You must be Brandy," she said and hugged me too.

Her home had floor-to-ceiling windows facing the street in the front of the house, fourteen-foot ceilings, and a double parlor off the main hall entrance. There was a grand staircase in the hall entrance that led to the second floor. The long, wide entry hall was tastefully furnished with art, a thin table with a Tiffany lamp, a hall tree to accommodate guests' coats, and a lawyer's style four-level bookcase a little farther down along the wall.

She led us into the double parlor where two facing sofas were upholstered in a soft linen in front of a beautiful white marble fireplace. There were two chairs at one end of the sofas facing the fireplace. A large coffee table sat between the seating area with a carved top suggesting it could be a treasure from the Far East. The dining room had a mirrored Parson's table and mirrored sideboard embellished with gold leaf. The crystal chandelier over the dining table was a gold

Murano glass with matching wall sconces on either side of the sideboard. Off the double parlor she used for a living room and through the dining room I could see a newly renovated, all white kitchen with white Carrera marble countertops.

"Can I get you a beer or a glass of wine? I'm having a glass of Pinot Grigio…you?" Esme asked us. We both accepted a glass of what she was having. "Have a seat and I'll be right back," she said. When she got up, Sparkler followed her to the kitchen.

"That's three glasses," I said. "I'll come help you."

Jiff sat on one of the sofas with Blast, scratching him behind the ears.

"I'm so sorry about your sister and Ian," I said. "Jiff and I want to help you any way we can."

"I appreciate it," she said pulling out two more glasses and pouring from an already opened bottle. "I know this wasn't an accident no matter what they come back and say," she added.

I put my hand on her arm. There was a closeness I immediately felt with Esme.

"Blast and Sparkler. Cute names. I'm guessing that it has something to do with the fireworks business," I said.

"Yes. Sophie brought him here asking if I'd watch him overnight. Our parents have a vet clinic, and we both usually board our pets with them if we go out of town or have a party. They left for a two-week cruise the day before the holiday weekend and the clinic is closed until they return. I thought that was odd since she always kept Blast home, up in their bedroom, door closed and playing rock and roll music for him if it was only for one night. Downstairs had more of the same music pumping out over Ian's home entertainment system. Blast was fine as long as he didn't hear the fireworks," she said.

"I put Meaux in my room with music if I have to leave him." I said. "If I'm home he just sits on top of me and doesn't seem too bothered by them."

"Sophie was always afraid Blast would hear them if she boarded him. She didn't mind leaving him at my parents' vet clinic when she and Ian travelled because my parents took him home with them. We all took turns spoiling him when they went on vacation."

We picked up the glasses and headed back to the double parlor where Jiff sat. Once we were all seated, Jiff made a toast to Sophie and Ian saying we would help find out what really happened.

"Esme, my firm handles a lot of criminal cases so I have a very good investigator along with a secret weapon," Jiff said.

"Secret weapon?" I asked.

"You," he said looking at me. "You and I have solved a couple of unusual crimes together and I think this one qualifies, don't you think?" Then he said to Esme, "Brandy has an uncanny ability to see what others miss. She sees what others overlook."

"I don't think this was an accident," I said.

"Neither do I," Esme added tearing up and wiping her eyes with a tissue she had in a pocket.

"That makes three of us in agreement," added Jiff. "I got a letter from Ian yesterday in the mail asking me to speak with you regarding a contract for his new business. Here it is. You need to read it."

He handed the envelope to Esme.

When she finished, she said, "Yes, Ian and Sophie told me they were asking you to write the contract. I was going to recommend it if they didn't say that's what they planned. I knew Angie would throw a hissy if I were to do it. I'm sure Ian wanted to keep me at an arm's distance so as not to cause friction among them. Angie and Phillip might think," she paused before continuing, "really, only Angie might think, I would protect the interests of my sister and husband more than theirs."

"Angie is Phillip's wife, and Phillip was Ian's partner, right?" I asked.

Esme nodded still looking at the letter in her hand.

"Was there friction with Angie and the new business?" Jiff asked.

"Angie had friction over everything with everyone.

She was insanely jealous of anyone that took Phillip's attention away from her for a second," Esme said. "She hounded Phillip and Ian to hire her brother, Freddie, to help with the firework displays. I think she wanted him around to keep an eye on Phillip when she wasn't there and report back to her if he noticed anything going on," she said.

"Anything going on? Like what?" I asked.

"Angie believed Phillip was having an affair," Esme said. "She called me and asked me if he was. I guess because I'm a divorce attorney and she might have thought he'd come to seek my professional services. Maybe she thought I'd tell her if he did."

"What did you tell her?" I asked.

"I gave her the same advice I give all my clients in family law. I suggested she and her husband talk to a counselor to work through any issues they might be having," Esme said. "That didn't go over well. She hung up on me saying she was calling Ian next."

"Do you know if she called Ian?" Jiff asked.

"She did. I called Ian immediately to give him a head's up, but she had already called him before she called me. She is such a little liar. She told Ian that Phillip was acting strange and moving assets to LLC's. She also said she was hiring an investigator, but I think she was having Freddie follow Phillip," Esme said.

"How can you be so sure Phillip wasn't seeing

someone?" Jiff asked. He held up his hands at once adding, "Just being the devil's advocate looking for motives. Who had the most to gain, and who had the most to lose?"

"Well, I know Phillip wasn't seeing anyone...except me," she said.

Jiff and I looked back and forth to each other then back to Esme. We sat there in stunned silence for a moment not knowing what to ask or say next.

When she saw the look on our faces she hurriedly added, "We were not, are not, having an affair. He came to my office to ask what he needed to do to protect himself and start divorce proceedings. I told him, and then, I recommended another attorney for him to see. I didn't want to represent him or be involved in that mess. Phillip is a nice, sweet guy. He didn't belong with Angie. He started confiding in me, but we never crossed that line. He told me Angie's jealousy had become intolerable and he wanted out of the marriage. He said the things to me, well, you know, like 'too bad we never gave it a chance,' 'we might have made a good go of it,' that sort of thing. We only met at my office twice when he wanted to talk, for coffee, but it never went further than that. I suggested he might want to give Ian and Sophie a warning on the fact he might be divorcing Angie."

"Wow," I said. "Did Ian know this? Why would he

start a new business venture with that going on?"

Esme said she didn't know if Ian knew Phillip wanted to file for divorce, but given their friendship and closeness, she believed he had to have known. What she did say was, "Ian said Phillip was in charge of the operational end of the fireworks business while he set up meetings and sold the idea of his firework displays to counties and parishes along the Gulf Coast from Grand Isle to Mobile. It was very successful for the two or three times a year different municipalities hired them. Ian hired and trained more people to work setting up and lighting the displays when needed."

"Didn't they both also work for the EPA?" Jiff asked.

"I'll get to that," Esme said. I think it's important for you to know the setup from the beginning—when Ian and Phillip built the fireworks business—up until now."

"Go on," Jiff said.

"Both of them wanted to keep the fireworks business because they loved it. Ian had hoped if either of them had kids one day, they might love it enough to take it over. Since neither couple had children and it didn't look like any were planned for the foreseeable future, they hired a receptionist or Girl Friday to help with bookkeeping, taking messages...that sort of thing," Esme said.

"I'm guessing that didn't go over well with Angie?" I asked.

"That gal never warmed her chair before Angie started complaining about her. Then Angie started browbeating Phillip to hire Freddie full time saying he could do what the girl did plus help with some displays when they needed an extra."

"Did they hire him?" Jiff asked.

"Yes, unfortunately. Freddie flunked out of high school, never went to college or served, so no training in anything except he rode with bikers for a few years," she said.

"Bikers? Like a cycling club?" I asked.

"Obviously, you've never met Freddie. He was a biker, like a motorcycle biker. I'm not sure of any of the particulars, and I'm a little prejudiced against him. He was in a chapter or a Westbank club—that's what Phillip said they prefer to be called instead of a gang. Phillip said he fell off his bike or ran into the other riders one too many times so they kicked him out. He has very poor vision," she said.

"A bad biker? Like in a bad steering biker?" I asked.

"I think so. Anyway, Angie's father was the Fire Chief in St. Tammany Parish, north of the lake, and Freddie grew up knowing the ins and outs of fire investigation and explosives. I can't tell you if Freddie was any good at the job or if he knew enough to be dangerous. Phillip said Freddie never officially worked for the fire department and that's probably the only reason the bikers let him in their gang is they thought he had a skill they could use. They probably thought he would make a good arsonist."

"Well, Ian and Phillip spent time in the military and worked as a two-man team in Explosive Ordinance Disposal or EOD. Those two should have seen whether or not Freddie was worth taking on," Jiff said.

"You're right, but by this time, Angie was becoming more jealous and disruptive in everything," Esme said. "Ian didn't think Freddie would last long because there was so much manual labor, so he agreed."

There was a moment when Esme seemed to ponder what to say next.

"Go on," Jiff prodded.

"You should know, Phillip asked me to marry him when he got back from Afghanistan."

"So you two were a thing?" I asked. "That couldn't have made Angie happy."

"It wasn't enough to be a thing. I don't think she ever knew. While they were deployed, Phillip wrote to me a lot. I believe he thought we were a thing. It was more like a pen pal thing, and Ian probably encouraged it since Phillip never had a girlfriend. We had never gone on a date.

"I started college after they were in the military

serving in the sand box. I finished a four-year program in three. After their tour, they returned to go to law school on the GI bill and I had caught up with them. We were all at Tulane Law School together," she said.

"Yes, Esme was the smart one finishing undergraduate in record time," Jiff said. "I took my time so I could make good grades."

"I liked Phillip. Maybe if we had met later, after school or after I had started my practice, I would have had time for his attentions. I just didn't back then," Esme said. "When he met Angie, she pounced on him. Phillip never had a chance with anyone after that."

"What about this new business?" Jiff asked. "Can you tell us why Ian would want to start a new business with Phillip when all that stuff with Angie was... is... going on?"

"There was more to this new venture than I can tell you. All I know is that Ian and Phillip were both really smart and they worked for the EPA. Something was going on there, but I don't know what it was. I'm sure Sophie knew. She was involved with the lab they were setting up. The only thing Ian told me when we spoke of any contracts was, and I quote, "Whatever you write up as a contract, please keep Angie out of it so she has no legal claim to the business. I want it written so if something happens to Phillip or their marriage, his interests and management of the company will transfer back into the business unless he has children. Then it goes to them when they reach twenty-five."

"Oh, do you know where we could find Ian's computer," I asked.

"No, unless it's in his car or his office. Ask Phillip, but I think you should talk to Phillip when Angie is not around, if you can manage that. Ian trusted him and I trust him. Here's his cell phone number," she said writing it down on a note pad on the coffee table. "Phillip is a great guy, and always had Ian's back. I wish I knew why he wasn't there with Ian on that barge. Someone took Ian and the explosives out there," Esme said. "You should ask him who did that."

Chapter Six

Tuesday p.m.

W HEN WE GOT to Jiff's car, I saw Anthony had finally called me back and left a message.

It said, "It's Ant-knee. Call me."

OMG, I thought, even he said his name that way.

Getting information out of Anthony was going to test my fortitude. He didn't leave a time that's good to call back. I might play phone tag with him like this for days. I took a chance and hit the call back button. All the stars in the heavens were in alignment.

"Hey, Brandy," Anthony answered.

"How did you know it was me?" I asked him.

"I put your number in my contact list," he said. "Don't you do that?"

"Yes, I save names in contacts. Jeffrey said you might be able to help me find someone I'm looking for. I want to find and talk to the guy who was squatting in a building you cleaned. The guy who told you he saw dynamite? Remember him?"

"Yeah, I remember him, but he got moved out while I was working there," Anthony said.

"Wait. What? What do you mean, he got moved out? I thought he was homeless," I said.

"He is homeless. He did have a ride of his own. It was some old motorcycle. Every so often the police get called to roust the homeless out of buildings they are living in. You know, it's a fire hazard. I told the owner he was in there and I guess he sent the police," he said.

"Great, there goes my witness," I said.

"Witness?" Anthony asked.

"Yes, we think the guy who came to get the dynamite might be responsible for that 4th of July explosion on the lake. I was hoping he could give us a description of who he saw. It might be who did the crime," I said.

"Sorry if it messed you up. I'm sorry I got him booted out of there," Anthony said.

"Wait, who is the owner you called? Do you remember his name?" I asked.

"I have to check my contacts on my job sheet for the name of the person I talked to, but I can tell you where it is," Anthony said.

By now I had him on speakerphone so Jiff could hear him. I asked him to go ahead and give me the directions.

"That building is on Richard Street right off Tchoupitoulas, on the lake side of Tchoup, not the river side. If you are driving down Tchoupitoulas from the I-10, turn right on Richard, and it's at the next corner. It's the only vacant building on that street with a FOR LEASE sign in front of it right now."

"Great. Thanks Anthony," I said. "Can I call you if I have any more questions?"

"Sure."

"Hey, one more thing. If you spot your homeless guy, will you call or text me and let me know where I can find him before you call the owner or police, please?"

"I've got your number, so yeah, I can do that. It's possible I might run into him again, squatting in another vacant building. Most of the graffiti I'm hired to do is on vacant buildings. He seemed like a nice guy, just down on his luck. I'm kinda sorry I told the building owner he was in there. The guy I talked to was a jerk. If I find him, I'll let you know," Anthony said and hung up.

"I'll get my investigator on this," Jiff said. "She'll track down the owner of that building and background info on Phillip and Angie before we talk to Phillip." Jiff made a call to his investigator and then suggested we grab dinner somewhere. He suggested La Crêpe Nanou since we were uptown and I agreed. Crêpe Nanou was a little French restaurant that specialized in all kinds of crêpes, mussels, and my favorite French wine. I loved their crabmeat crêpe and French Onion soup.

I made a call to Dante to let him know about the building where the dynamite was seen. Taylor answered, and when he realized it was me said there were two sets of human remains found in the fire, still unidentified. He added, "Ian Saucier's, partner, Phillip Wilson, took out a million-dollar life insurance policy on Ian and Sophie."

"Wait. What?" I asked Taylor.

"Your friends' partner is looking good for this. We'll probably bring him in for questioning tonight or tomorrow," Taylor said. "But you didn't hear it from me."

Before I got off the phone with Taylor, Michelle, Jiff's investigator, called back and confirmed some of the information Taylor just told me.

"It seems the owner of that building is Up in Smoke, LLC. That means Ian and Phillip own it and the contact person listed for all inquiries and on the Louisiana Secretary of State's website is Phillip Wilson," Jiff said.

"They own the building?" I asked with a million questions buzzing in my brain like a hive of bees. "That homeless man might have seen Phillip with the dynamite."

"I can't believe Phillip would be rude, let alone hide dynamite and use it to kill Ian," Jiff said, "That's preposterous, although Michelle just told me something unsettling. She confirmed Phillip took out a million-dollar life insurance policy on Ian Saucier and one on Sophie Saucier about two weeks ago," he said.

"Taylor just told me the same thing. No time for dinner," I said. "We have to talk to Phillip. Call him. Get him to meet us somewhere, not at his home or office. Tell him it's important for him to leave his home or office…now."

"Sounds urgent," Jiff said calling Phillip.

"Phillip has a lot of questions to answer, and we won't be able to talk to him if the police arrest him," I said. "You know, Anthony didn't make Phillip sound like the nice guy you and Esme are making him out to be."

"You met Phillip. He's one of the nicest guys I know, always has been. He's very centered and calm, which made him good with explosives. Maybe someone else talked to Anthony, like one of the guys they hired to set up and light the fireworks. I'm surprised the police haven't pounced on him yet," Jiff said. "Life insurance policies are usually a red flag. I hope he has a good attorney."

Phillip took Jiff's call and agreed to meet us without Angie at Jiff's office. We raced back to Canal Place and up to the suite of Heinkel and Heinkel to make sure we were there before Phillip arrived. Most, if not all, of the staff had already gone home. One or two lights were on in the offices of associates burning the midnight oil researching. I waited for Phillip in the reception area while Jiff went to open up his office.

Phillip was a tall, fit, soldier-looking kinda guy from the way he conducted himself. His military style haircut gave him away along with the fact that he always appeared to be standing at attention. He was incredibly polite, shaking my hand when I extended mine, calling me ma'am at the end of every sentence. He wore chino slacks pressed with a crease sharp enough to cut steak and a heavily starched, cotton, button-down shirt that didn't have a wrinkle in it. It was unlikely he just changed his clothes, since he told Jiff he was at his office a few minutes away from here. He had to have had that shirt on all day.

"I'm sorry we're meeting under these circumstances, Phillip," I said. "I didn't know Ian or Sophie. I was supposed to meet them at their barbecue. Jiff knew the three of you, I believe, from law school, right?"

"Yes, ma'am, we do…did… all know each other since high school actually. In fact, I might need Jiff's legal counsel since I think the police are going to question me," he said.

"Well, Jiff's in his office. I'll show you," I said leading him through the maze of corridors and offices, many of which were dark by now.

After a friendly reunion of handshakes and man hugs, Jiff and Phillip sat down and Jiff started by asking if Phillip had an attorney.

Phillip answered, "I've never practiced, but I'm getting concerned I might need one where this involves Ian, Sophie, and the business we're in. Sophie's sister, Esme, has always done any filing for us that was required to set up our business entities, but she doesn't handle cases like this."

"I think you should retain counsel," Jiff said. "You know I handle criminal defense, and I can represent you unless you have someone else in mind. Let's just say for the purpose of this meeting, I do represent you, so anything you tell me is in confidence. Brandy just found out the police are going to want to talk to you. Please don't speak with them unless you have me or legal representation with you."

"I didn't do anything wrong. Ian and I have been friends for years. We're closer than brothers, you know that. We fought in Afghanistan together...had each other's back..."

Jiff held up both hands to Phillip and said, "I know that, but we think..." Jiff looked at me, "Brandy and I saw both explosions, so we think these are homicides. Along with homicides come the police with a lot of questions for everyone close to the victims."

"Then, please represent me. I wouldn't know who

else to ask. Ian and I took jobs with the EPA right out of law school. It paid well and we were happy to be offered employment somewhere. While they liked the fact Ian and I had law degrees, we technically never practiced," he said. "You're right, I'm sure the police will want to talk to me. I can imagine how this looks."

"I will represent you. Let's talk first and then I'll get you to sign a contract saying I legally represent you. The number I called you on earlier is my cell number to reach me anytime, day or night. Do not speak to anyone, police, private investigator, anyone asking questions, without me present. Understand?" Jiff asked. "Here's my card with the office number if you can't reach me. Call them and tell them it's important."

"Yes, I understand. Thanks," Phillip said.

"Brandy works with me on cases. She's not an attorney but she is a trusted member of our team here. If you don't want her in here, that's fine. I do think you could benefit from her hearing the facts. She never met Sophie or Ian. She will have fresh eyes on this and she sees things that get left out or others miss," Jiff said.

"No, please stay," Phillip said. "I need all the help I can get to protect me and find out who did this to Ian and Sophie."

"I'm going to ask you some hard questions, and you need to be honest with me," Jiff asked.

"I have nothing to hide," Phillip said.

"We spoke to Esme, and she said you two were something of an item when you came back from Afghanistan. Right?" Jiff asked.

"Yes, and no. I wrote to her and she wrote me back. She started law school with us, so unless you count study groups or sitting in a classroom together as dating, we never had one. I was young. I was lonely over there and she was like Ian's little sister. She wrote to both of us all the time. Ian had Sophie…well, you get it."

"What about now? What is your relationship with her now?" Jiff asked.

"We're friends, always have been. She's easy to talk to, and she's known me since I was a kid, teenager really. I like her, but we're not having an affair or anything like that, if that's what you're asking," Phillip said and hesitated, looking down at his hands. "I have talked to her about filing for a divorce from my wife but it's not because I'm having an affair with Esme or anyone. She recommended I find another attorney since she's friends with all of us."

"That's good advice. Have you filed for divorce yet?" Jiff asked.

"No. I haven't called the attorney Esme recommended," he said. "I was going to wait until after the 4th because things have been so crazy with the firework contracts we had and getting the new business set up. I planned to talk to Ian and ask him to hold off putting my name on the lab business until after I divorced Angie."

"A divorce can take up to two years or longer if she contests it. Are you aware of that?" Jiff asked.

"Yes. I knew it was going to be an acrimonious divorce from my wife. She's difficult at best, and I'm anticipating this is not going to be amicable. I trusted Ian and Sophie to let me work in the business and add me as a partner when I finalized the divorce," Phillip said.

"Do you think Ian and Sophie would have done that... set it up to avoid dealing with Angie? Would they want to stay out of it?" Jiff asked.

"Most definitely they would have done it. I trusted them. They trusted me. They knew Angie was very jealous and constantly accused me of having affairs. She had even accused me of having an affair with Sophie...which is not, I repeat...not true. Ian knew how Angie could be. Ian was a good friend and tried to warn me off of her when I started dating her, but I didn't listen. Like I said, we were close. I tried to keep it from getting ugly."

"Phillip, this is already ugly," Jiff said.

I looked at Jiff, who let out a long breath, then put his elbows on his desk and rested his chin on his folded hands. This was his thinking pose. When he didn't have a desk to rest both elbows on, he used one hand to hold an elbow and the other to rest his chin.

Phillip said, "Ian, Sophie, along with Esme were like my family. While the work itself was boring, it wasn't when I worked with Ian. It's hard to believe Angie is trying to ruin this for all of us. It seems she got worse around the time we started talking about setting up the lab."

"Did Ian or Sophie know how Angie felt about the lab, or that she accused the two of you?" Jiff asked.

"I'm sure of it. Angie was not one to suffer in silence. She's insanely jealous of the least little thing. She involves anyone who will listen and take her side. If she can't gain their support, they become her enemy and are taking my side. This is why I just want out of the marriage. Ian and Sophie have been great to us. They didn't deserve how Angie is…how she treated them. It was embarrassing."

"Well, this isn't good, but we'll work around it. There is something else. You took out a life insurance policy on Ian and Sophie? What prompted that?" Jiff asked.

"That was Ian's idea. Ian suggested we take out a life insurance policy on each other for business reasons, should something happen to one of us. Of course, we didn't put any of this agreement in writing or in an email for the life insurance on each other. What prompted this had to do with what was going on with a lab we were sending our samples to in our current positions at the EPA," Phillip answered.

"What was going on with the samples sent to that lab?" Jiff asked.

"Samples we collected in certain areas of the wetlands were always fine. One or two were said to have gotten lost so we had to resend. If we inquired about the samples to see when we'd get the results, we received remarks from the lab like, 'if it was something important, I would have called you'. They never called us. We've always had to call them for a follow-up. It became clear, the message was, 'Don't call us. We'll call you," Phillip said.

"Did any of the other agents say they had the same issues?" Jiff asked.

"Funny you should ask that. Ian and I felt like we were being singled out so we asked one or two of the other agents if theirs would be conveniently misplaced or lost from the same general area. The answer was, yes. Ian and I brought this to the attention of our Director, and we were told that he'd talk to the lab but we still had to use that same lab, same as always, for the samples from our area. Nothing changed except it seemed the lab started sending us the same typed results over and over...nothing conclusive in the way of toxins. Only one lab was processing all samples from this one area. After we brought this to the Director's attention, that lab still returned clean results on the work we sent them, only we discovered it wasn't results on the samples we submitted. Ian and I maintained a log of what we sent and started testing those ourselves as a follow-up. That's when we found the toxins in what we tested and none in those that were returned from the labs."

"You think you and Ian discovered something illegal going on?" Jiff asked.

"Absolutely. All the samples we tested were heavy with toxins. Have you heard of fracking?"

"Yes. Isn't that where oil companies drill from one location underground to get to the oil somewhere else?"

"Oil or gas. It's been mostly used in areas with a higher rock concentration. We're on marsh here, but there were trials years ago that didn't produce results they wanted so fracking was discontinued. It seems the idea was abandoned, but not before continuing damage was left behind, leaking contaminants into the area," he said.

Some of the toxins that tested positive are not only harmful to the environment, but to the bodies of water they invade, leaving a toxic footprint that is growing and could soon reach the Gulf of Mexico," Phillip explained. "We overheard other agents say they found harmful levels in different areas and not one lab that has tested our samples has ever come back saying there is a problem. Ian and I got nervous so that's when we decided to do our own tests on the same samples we sent to the labs. We checked it multiple times, individually and together."

"Why didn't you go back to the Director?" I asked.

"Because the Director is Angie's uncle. He's her dad's brother, Uncle on the take, I've been calling him," Phillip said. "I only called him that when I was with Ian. His real name is Harvey Finklestein. He got Ian and I pushed through for these jobs. Do you see the mess we could be in by blowing the whistle? That's why Ian wanted life insurance on each of us. If something happened to either of us, there'd be an investigation."

"Okay, but how would the Director know what you suspected? Didn't you just say he looked into it, and then samples started coming back clean?" Jiff asked. "Could a co-worker have overheard or maybe the Director asked the other employees if they had similar issues."

"Yes. Even after he looked into it, all samples continued to come back clean. All the samples came back as if they had been scrubbed, they were so clean. That, in and of itself, was highly unusual. Ian and I were careful never to discuss the issues on any site we worked on, and we stopped chatting about it unless we were sure we were alone. We especially didn't talk about any of it around Angie. I was afraid she'd slip and say something to her dad or her uncle," Phillip said.

"Why were you concerned about that?" I asked.

"Something was up. Ian and I had confirmed it about that lab. Angie is a big eavesdropper and is always snooping around. She could have heard Ian and I talking about the results we found compared to the lab results. She leaned on me to hire her brother Freddie to work for us. I told her he wasn't a good fit and that it was up to Ian," he said. "I didn't think Ian would ever go for it, but I underestimated his compassion for all things family."

"When I told him the brother could be watching us, Ian said, 'Hide his glasses and he won't see a thing.' Freddie wore really thick eyeglasses. Seems he was teased about it his whole life."

Jiff started laughing and said, "That sounds like Ian."

Phillip went on to say, "Ian wasn't worried because he said Freddie would probably quit when he had to do real work, like lifting all the boxes of fireworks for our events. But he didn't quit. He didn't do much work either. Freddie always had to get a temporary helper to assist him, another guy covered in tats. Those guys were old gang buddies of Freddie's and they did all the heavy lifting. I'm fed up with Angie and her whole family."

"What kinda tats? Anthony said the homeless guy

in your building had a lot of tats. Looked like gang tats," I said.

"I'm not down on tattoos. I have one from the military. Angie's got one on each wrist. But the guys Freddie brings around, including Freddie, are covered in them, so you know they don't have nine-to-five jobs," Phillip said. "They look like gang tattoos but I'm not an expert on those either. I just know gang members always seem to be covered in ink."

"Are you familiar with a building you own with Ian on Richard Street near Religious Street off Tchoupi-toulas?" Jiff asked.

"Yes, sort of. I haven't been to it since we bought it, but I know where it is."

"Did you recently hire someone to have graffiti cleaned from it?" Jiff asked.

"Yes, it's too big for the lab so Ian suggested we lease part of the space to help offset the expenses with another business until we were ready to expand. What is this about?" Phillip asked.

Jiff held up a finger indicating he would answer these questions in a second, then asked, "Did Anthony, the guy cleaning the building for you, call and tell you there was a homeless guy living in there?" Jiff pressed on.

"I don't remember that, no," Phillip said. "I think it was either Sophie or Angie who actually hired the cleaner."

"Did you call the police to have any homeless or squatters removed from that building?" Jiff asked.

"No, why would I? If they were there, I didn't know about it," Phillip said. "I saw enough guys I served with fall down on their luck after returning from overseas. I could have been one of them. If the guy was or wasn't a veteran, I would have tried to help him find somewhere safe to live, or given him some cash to find a place, not thrown him out."

"Did you have dynamite stored at that location? Richard Street?" Jiff asked.

"Dynamite? Not that I know of. Why would you ask...oh, the explosion with Ian," Phillip said. "That was more than the fireworks we had scheduled to go off that blew up Ian. I saw that barge."

I said, "Anthony, the guy who cleaned the building, said the homeless man told him there was dynamite stored there. The homeless guy told Anthony he read it on the boxes and some men came and moved all the boxes out right before the graffiti cleaning started."

"Not me, and I know it wasn't Ian either. We don't deal in dynamite or anything that is considered military grade explosives. I had enough of that stuff while I served, and Ian did too. The biggest thing I want to deal with is a blast. OK, some blasts are big, but not the size that could kill you, like one stick of dynamite could. Our fireworks can blow off a finger or hand, cause hearing loss or burn you pretty bad if you are not careful, but kill you? No. We are not licensed for handling commercial grade explosives, and like I said, I had enough of that stuff in the military," Phillip said pounding a clenched fist on Jiff's desk in front of him.

That was the most adamant I had heard Phillip talk since he came to meet us. He was always confident and polite. There was no mistaking his position on dynamite. He was very clear.

"Oh, one last thing. Who brought Ian out to the barge that night?" Jiff asked. "Do you know?"

"It was Freddie. They left the office together and Ian drove. I heard Ian tell Freddie they were going to use Ian's party boat to bring the fireworks out to the barge. He told Freddie he didn't have to sit on the barge but he had to wait at their boathouse and come back to get him when the display was over. That's my understanding of what was supposed to happen." There was a pause and he added, "I should have gone with him and sent Freddie to bring the additional inventory to the barge on the river."

"Then you both might have been killed," I said. "Have you seen or talked with Freddie?"

"No, not willingly. I try to avoid him," Phillip said. He paused then added, "Hey, thanks for seeing me on short notice and staying so late. I feel a little better about having talked about this now."

Jiff wrapped up the interview and told Phillip he would represent him. He sent two copies of his firm's Client/Attorney Agreement to Represent to his printer and had Phillip sign both before he left, giving him one copy to take with him.

After escorting Phillip to the elevator, I returned to Jiff's office to find him leaning back in his chair, looking up at the ceiling with his feet on his desk. He sat upright and let out a big exhale.

"Well, what do you think of all that?" Jiff asked me.

"I think someone is setting him up," I said.

Chapter Seven

Tuesday p.m.

IT WAS TOO late for dinner, so Jiff and I went back to my house. I opened a bottle of Pinot Grigio from my small wine collection, sliced some Monterey Jack cheese and Granny Smith apples, putting it all on a plate with a variety of crackers. This is my preferred meal on nights Jiff and I don't go out to dinner together, when I eat alone, or am not in the mood to cook. This was as good a time as any to introduce Jiff to my "go to" dinner for one, now two. Meaux loves cheese too, so I also pull out some string cheese which I keep on hand to train him when we practice commands like come, stay, lie down, or sit. The really hard commands, like bark whenever you feel like it, jump on the furniture or don't listen to me, do whatever you want, don't require much in the way of training. He has taught himself those. Tonight, however, was just reward night for him with no training or commands to follow. I could get Meaux to do anything for cheese. Like owner—like dog.

Jiff and I sat on the sofa next to each other with the plate of snacks on the coffee table in front of us. Meaux was at my feet, staring at us. We fell into a routine where we sipped our wine, nibbled on cheese, then fed Meaux a piece. If we didn't repeat this fast enough I would get a paw on my leg. I knew what he was thinking from the pensive stare he was giving us... *I wish they would skip steps one and two and just give me the cheese.* Finally, after four or five cycles of sip, nibble, feed cheese to Meaux, I said, "A couple of things occurred to me if Phillip was having an affair with Ian's wife."

Jiff looked at me, handed Meaux another bite of string cheese and said, "Go on. I'm trying not to ask these same questions myself. I'd feel better if you do. Just shout 'em on out."

"Remember, I'm just being the devil's advocate. If we can't poke holes in this, the police will and they will arrest him," I said.

Jiff nodded.

"One, if Phillip was having an affair with Sophie, maybe he wanted Ian out of the picture to run off with her," I said.

"No," Jiff said shaking his head for the additional effect.

I ignored him.

"Two, if Angie thought Phillip was having an affair with Sophie," I said and held up my hand like a traffic cop to stop Jiff from another verbal response, "and it seems she did or at least told others she thought so, then she might want Sophie out of the picture bad enough to actually act on it," I said and then Jiff cut me off.

"Angie wanted Sophie out of the picture bad enough to try to burn down Sophie's house with Sophie in it?" he asked.

"Maybe. We've talked to two people who told us how insanely jealous she is," I said.

"I'll go after her with everything I've got if she is involved…" he said.

"Wait. I have two more. Three, maybe Phillip isn't the incredibly nice guy I really think he is, but wanted Ian out of the picture to claim the new business for himself and Angie."

Jiff said, "No way. Sorry, what else you got?"

"I'm not all in on number three either. Four, could Angie and Phillip have been working to get rid of Ian and Sophie? It seems Angie and Sophie took turns working in the business UP IN SMOKE, so Angie could have known a lot more about ordering, the life insurance, etc. than she's letting on, especially since her brother, Freddie, was there to snoop around when she wasn't," I said.

"Okay, only the half of four that has Angie in it is a

possibility. I can see that. What else?" he said.

"That's all I've got," I said.

"Okay, Five. Take Phillip out of number Four and I think that's what we're looking at" Jiff said. "Esme and Phillip both sound like they don't think much of Angie. I almost don't want to meet her, but I think it might be best if you could talk to her by yourself?"

"Bawk, bawk, bawk," I said making the sound of a chicken. "No, your Grand Chicken-ness." I bowed at the waist while doing this hand roll thing like he was a Grand Poobah or king of something. "I'm not going to see her alone. I doubt she'd even open the door and let me in. You…you would have a better chance with her. You could charm her, because you're incredibly handsome with great manners women find intoxicating. Have I ever told you that?" I asked feeding him a piece of cheese and nodding, hoping he would nod back in agreement.

"Okay. Nice try with the flattery; however, we chickens will go together to question Angie at her coop," Jiff said.

"Okay, in my head, that was going to end with me *not* going with you," I said.

"I bet it did, but no," he said laughing while he gave Meaux another piece of cheese.

"I think he's had enough. He'll go on strike and never will eat his food if you fill him up on cheese. He loves, loves, loves cheese," I said petting and kissing

Meaux's head when he jumped up in my lap after I slowed down handing him bites.

"You should leave Meaux with Isabella at my place when you think you're gonna be late. My housekeeper feeds Isabella dinner and walks her three times a day, four times if I'm going to be late. She'd walk Meaux with Isabella. They would love that."

"I like coming home and taking care of him. I don't want someone else walking and feeding my dog every day. Suzanne lives here with us and likes having a dog in the house. She's here most of the day with him and will let him out if I'm running late. But that's not often, and I love coming home and having him greet me after a long day." I hugged Meaux while he stared at the coffee table to see how much cheese was left on the plate. "I hope he loves me as much as he loves cheese," I said.

"Well, we could all move in together, and then you could come home when you want to and if you needed my housekeeper to take care of Meaux, then you would have that option available," he said. He wasn't looking at me while he took another piece of cheese on a cracker for himself.

"Are you suggesting that you, Isabella and your housekeeper move in here with me, Suzanne and Meaux? In our super small, barely two-bedroom, one-bath apartment? It might be a little tight, and I don't think Suzanne wants to share her room with your housekeeper."

"Well, if that's the only way it will work," he said. "Maybe my housekeeper would agree to sleep on your sofa?"

I gave Jiff my head tilt like the one Meaux gives me when he's trying really hard to understand what I'm saying.

"What I'm asking is, shouldn't we be planning to live together, or planning to buy a house together, or planning a wedding date together?"

"Wow. That's a lot of planning," I said, a little overwhelmed by everything he just mentioned, but the wedding word really stuck in my head. I wondered, did I hear him right?

"In what order do you want to squeeze in all that planning? Remember, we're working on double homicides, possible insurance fraud, arson and a long list of possible felonies I haven't even thought of yet, plus I have a job, and you do too."

"Yes. I want us to do all that stuff. So I have to ask you something," Jiff asked.

"Ask," I said. Meaux looked from Jiff to me and back to Jiff.

"Brandy Alexander, do you want to marry me?" he asked.

My heart felt like it was going to jump out of my chest. I felt the ground move, birds sang, bells rang, and yet I sat there like a mute. The question and the way it was phrased made me stop and think, was this a fact finding mission? He asked did I want to marry him, not, will I marry him? Semantics, yes, but just to be clear, what was he asking? I didn't want to reply ahead of the magic moment.

"I do want to marry you," I finally heard the words leave my lips. "I think I need to confer with Meaux since this means a life change for him too."

"Meaux, will you marry me if she will marry me?" Jiff asked petting his head.

Ah, finally the right question.

Meaux barked once, like he does when he thinks a question has to do with food. Meaux will always answer yes if he thinks food is involved.

"So, yes and yes! Let's start looking for a house together, and you decide when you want to set the date and what kind of wedding you want. I want what you want," he said kissing me. "You're making me the happiest and the luckiest man alive."

Part of me didn't like this happening at the same time we witnessed two of his friends going up in flames. I felt it was making us both consider our mortality and forcing us to move up decisions that should take more time to consider, perhaps involving more discussion. Or do life-changing events force decisions to be made in the moment?

"I'm not comfortable moving forward with wedding plans until we get this Ian and Sophie case resolved," I said.

"Yes, I know what you mean, and I feel the same way. But I don't want to put off moving forward in our life together, because I know that's what we both want. Let's just plan on looking for a place together in the meantime. I'll put my condo on the market, and we'll find a house you like, and we'll buy it together. My single and only requirement is it has to have a nice, big yard for Isabella and Meaux. Then, you can remodel it, fix it up, build one, I don't care what you want. As long as you're happy, I'm happy."

"It sounds like we're not moving forward, we're moving in fast forward," I said. "I need a little time to absorb and think about this. Did you know you were going to ask me this tonight?"

"No, I mean, yes, I knew I wanted to ask you all of this, but I'm not sure when I thought I should do it. Right now feels like the perfect time," Jiff said smiling from ear to ear.

"I'm happy, no ecstatic over all of it," I said. It was easy to get caught up in the moment seeing the elation all over Jiff's face.

"Who do you want to tell first? Do you want to call my parents?" he asked.

Uh oh. Wait. What? Tell people? Tell my family? No, no, no, no, no.

"I want to keep this between us for now. These should be our plans—plans we make together," I said hearing the tremble in my voice. I felt panic making my knees weak and tightening my stomach. My hands started to feel clammy. I was glad I was sitting down.

"Don't you want to tell our family and friends?" Jiff asked looking a little disappointed.

"I do want to tell your family and our friends," I said. "Isn't there a Marriage Protection Program, you know, like the Witness Protection Program that would keep it a secret from anyone you don't want finding out?" I said. "Like my family?"

"I don't think so," he said looking at me like I was crazy.

"There's no calling a do-over if we tell my family. There's no un-telling them once they find out, so let's make sure we're ready for them to start making my life miserable. I'm talking my family, not yours," I repeated. "Even if my mother only finds out an hour before the wedding, she can make that hour feel longer then the Bataan Death March. That lasted five, long, torturous days. That will look like a cake walk compared to one hour with my mother."

"So we can keep this between us until you're ready to tell your family," he said putting his arms around me and Meaux. "I'm just happy you both said yes."

"Jiff, I just want our ceremony to be special for the two of us. I want both of us to decide what we want in the way of a wedding, a place to live, when and how we are going to go about it. As soon as we make an announcement, we will be bombarded with questions on what our plans are, and suggestions on how we ought to go about it," I said. "I don't want any influence from my family especially, and they are bound to make their suggestions known and what they think if we don't use them. It will be nerve wracking and I might kill my mother in the process, winding up in prison. You would have to get the prison clergyman to perform the wedding ceremony through the thick, greenish, bulletproof glass over the phone while we are sitting down."

"Sitting down isn't necessarily a negative. Some of those Catholic masses can take forever," he said, not hiding a smile spreading over his face.

"No."

"So think about the plans you want to make, we'll make them, and then we'll announce it, okay?" he said.

"I was thinking we could elope, never mention it to my mother, and move to a foreign country where no one speaks English so she won't hound me the rest of my life for not having the wedding she thought I should have. That's all," I said.

Jiff laughed and hugged me saying, "C'mon, it won't be that bad."

I said, "You're right, it won't be that bad. It will be worse."

BY THE NEXT morning, before I went to work, my

stomach was so upset I couldn't eat or drink anything and felt like I was trying to hide a pregnancy instead of an engagement from my mother. Imagine if I was pregnant and trying to keep that from her. If my mother knew I was engaged and didn't tell her, she might never speak to me again. Wait…that in itself was not the worst thing that could happen. I mentally toyed with all the ways this might work for a few minutes.

Instead, I went to Suzanne's room to see if she was still up. She usually got home from work around 5:00 am She was still working at The Club Bare Minimum, but only until she graduated. She liked to call herself an exotic dancer, not a stripper. This was how she put herself through engineering school, which she was graduating from in a few more weeks. I heard her come in around the usual time I got up for my job. I was awake, or rather still awake and had not slept from the marriage plans I had made, or not made yet, with Jiff. I wanted to tell someone, and Julia was out of the question. She was like a human bullhorn and that news would be out on the airwaves before it completely left my lips.

Suzanne opened the door when I gently knocked. She was wearing sweats, her usually bedtime attire.

"Hey," I said. "Good morning."

"More like good night for me. You're up early," she said.

"Couldn't sleep. I have news, good news, and I

wanted to talk to you about it," I said.

"Talk to me or tell me?" she said looking a little confused. "At this time of night, I'm better at listening than talking. If I don't answer you, it means I fell asleep."

"Last night Jiff and I talked about moving in together, buying a house, and getting married," I said.

"That's a lot of talking," she said and a big smile spread across her face. "That's fantastic news. Sit down and tell me everything." She pointed to a chair in the corner for me to sit in while she plopped down on her bed.

"We… I… don't want to make any big announcements yet because I want to figure out what I want in the way of a wedding, a place to live…where to live," I said.

"I get it. You can't get the genie back in the bottle once you tell your mother. Telling Julia news of your engagement would spread faster than a California wildfire," Suzanne said. "Everyone will start weighing in unless you tell them to mind their own business, which they won't. Then, you will be in a big fight with…your mother for sure, maybe not Julia. She's clueless."

"You are so smart… and obviously clairvoyant…it scares me," I said.

"I'm happy for you, and your secret is safe with me until you announce it," she said.

"I don't know where to start. I told Jiff I wanted us to decide what we wanted, and then we'll announce it all, after I've made the arrangements."

"Sounds smart to me, but you know arrangements could take a year or longer to settle on. Can you keep it quiet that long?"

"A year?" I asked.

"Wait until your mother finds out," Suzanne said still smiling at my news. "Please let me be there when you tell her."

"You can be there, and you can even tell her because I won't be there. I think I'll write her a note and have you deliver it," I said. "Maybe I'll send her an email."

"Have you thought of eloping?" Suzanne asked laughing at my expense.

"Yes, that was my first thought and my second thought involved moving to a foreign country, someplace that doesn't speak English so she can't contact me," I said. "Why am I dreading having to deal with her when this should be one of the happiest days of my life?"

"It should be *the* happiest day of your life, and don't worry about her. This is your wedding. She had hers when she married your dad and had it again with your sister's wedding. You don't owe her anything after that fiasco she wanted to involve you in when your sister got married. Remember?" Suzanne asked.

"How could I forget?" I said.

"She is the way she is and she's not going to change anytime soon. Just send her an invitation after everything is the way you want it...think how happy your dad will be," she said, her smile spreading wider.

"Yes, my dad will be happy, but not as happy as he would be if I were marrying Dante," I said.

"Dante!" we both said at the same time.

"Oh, right. I really don't want to tell him," I said. "Would you tell him when you tell my mother?"

Suzanne crossed her arms over her chest and stood looking at me. The answer she wasn't saying was clearly no.

"Please?" I begged. "Name your price."

"You need to tell them both," she said very firmly, like she was correcting a child.

"Maybe he'll realize it's happening if I send him an invitation," I said.

"No, I think you should tell him BEFORE you tell your parents. Meet him for a drink. Get him a couple of strong ones first, then drop it on him, and leave," she said. "That's the best way to deliver that kinda news."

"Really?" I wondered if it could be that easy. "I can't use drinks with my mother. She's as mean as a snake when she's sober and like Attila the Hun after a couple of drinks. That won't work. I need to think of something else, and you need to help me."

Chapter Eight

Wednesday afternoon

S O, NOW I had my future to consider, which seemed to take up every waking moment in my life when I wasn't trying to figure out what happened to Ian and Sophie. I was silly-in-love happy.

Jiff and I were giddy together. We were constantly touching each other or smiling at nothing and just looking at each other for longer than usual. When we were around other people, they started noticing. I guess it's easy to spot two people in love.

It was during this secret phase of our engagement bliss we ran into Detective Hanky and Detective Taylor coming out of the criminal court building. I was waiting beside my car, on the driver's side, for Jiff. He ran inside to file a motion for one of his cases, and then we were going to dinner.

"Counselor," Hanky said trying to catch Jiff's attention just as he was leaving the building on his way to my car and my smiling face. She was hurrying down the steps in heels, waving her arms to get his attention. When Jiff didn't respond, Hanky screamed out at me, "Wait a minute. Brandy, wait up."

Detective Taylor followed her, unhurried yet keeping in step with Hanky. Hanky had trouble walking in high heels, let alone running in them. She more or less appeared to be jogging in place with her elbows moving in sync with her feet.

I looked at her with a toothy smile while Jiff turned to see who called him with an equally big grin on his face as he walked up to get in on the passenger side next to the curb.

"You two just win the lottery?" Detective Taylor asked as they both walked up at the same time.

"What?" I asked smiling. "Why do you ask?"

"What's with you two?" asked Hanky turning her head and eyeing us like a parakeet with one eye. It was the same way Woozie, our family housekeeper who raised me, always looked at me when she scrutinized something I was doing.

When we shrugged and said "Nothing," together. Hanky looked skeptical and Taylor kept staring. Then she asked, "Did you two just get married? Did you get some judge friend of yours to marry you?"

The smile disappeared from my face immediately and what felt like terror took its place. "No, why would you ask that?" Then I did my stupid nervous laugh my mother said made me sound like a hyena.

"You're both at the court house at the same time," she said.

"It's the criminal court house, not the civil district," Jiff answered.

"Criminal or civil," Hanky said, "any judge can marry you."

She was right. Hanky asking if we had a judge friend marry us made me think this might not be such a bad idea. We could get married, then announce it at the party. That would eliminate the entire wedding ordeal so we could continue being happy together without these socially awkward encounters with invasive questions. We'd be married. That would be it.

Detective Taylor was staring at me without blinking. Finally, he asked, "I thought you were going to call me if you talked to any of the family regarding the barge explosion and house fire. Did you talk to anyone?" If this was the look Taylor gave a suspect, then I never wanted to sit across the interrogation table from him.

"Right. We got nothing," I said. "You? ID any bodies in that fire?" I asked, trying to keep him on the defensive. It wasn't working. I still felt very uncomfortable in front of the two of them and was moving, awkwardly, reaching back for the handle on the car door.

"Not yet. Two, maybe three bodies, but we're not sure who they are yet. Do you have any idea why three bodies would be in that house?" he asked, still not blinking. It was now a stare.

I forced my lips together, hoping my mouth would turn down at the corners—a challenge when I wanted to smile like a clown—and shook my head no. Taylor never stopped staring at me. Hanky was looking back and forth from me to Jiff. Holding my mouth like this, trying to purse my lips into an upside-down smile, made my face feel like I was poised to give someone a little kiss, like a baby kiss goodbye.

Jiff jumped in and said, "I'm the counsel for Ian Saucier's partner, Phillip Wilson, in their fireworks company. Should you need to speak to him, please contact my office if you have any questions for him."

"Is he involved?" Hanky asked.

"Here's my card with my cell and office number," Jiff said by way of an answer to Hanky while trying to make a hasty exit.

As we left them standing there, I could hear Hanky saying to Taylor, "I bet they had a judge marry them."

Jiff and I got in my BMW and I couldn't drive away fast enough. I hit the gas pedal as hard as I dared without leaving burning rubber in front of the criminal court building on the corner of Tulane Avenue and Broad Street.

"Hey, slow down," Jiff said while attempting to fasten his seat belt in a hurry. "The jail for DUIs or Reckless Operation of a Vehicle is right next to the courthouse. They won't have far to take us if we get arrested."

"I want to get far away from those two before either one starts asking more questions," I said.

"Whoa! This is freaking you out a little, isn't it?" Jiff asked.

"More than a little. I'm not ready for this kind of gossip to bounce around," I said.

BEFORE THE BIG encounter with Hanky and Taylor, Jiff and I had decided it might be a good time to talk to Angie before the police got to her. We wanted to hear her answers on questions we had. From what Esme and Phillip had said about her, I expected a boatload of lies she was going to tell us and the police. Maybe we could get a jump on trying to figure out the truth. If Detective Taylor or Detective Hanky and I compared notes, maybe we'd catch her in a few.

I have to add, Jiff and I foolishly made the decision to see Angie Wilson on my lunch hour. When you are incredibly happy, you just can't see you've positioned yourself in the middle of a tunnel and the light heading straight at you is a freight train.

Angie Wilson answered the door with a scowl. It

only exaggerated the pinched features of her thin face. Her small, hard squinty eyes darted everywhere. She looked us both up and down checking us out without even a hint of discretion. She was a slender person, maybe five foot five. She wore an expensive looking sheath dress in beige with low-heeled matching beige pumps. She had shoulder-length, thin mousy brown hair and was twisting a faux strand of pearls she wore around her neck. She looked like she was at a casting call trying out for a role as a housewife from one of the TV sitcoms filmed in the 1950s or 1960s. The tattoos on the inside of each wrist suggested no one was ever going to call her back.

One wrist had a tattoo of a motorcycle heading at you with angel wings for handlebars. The other wrist had a skull and crossbones on it. One arm had a heart tattoo with her initials etched in the universal love motif, the "L" in the middle with what I was sure were Phillip's initials underneath. I also noticed a barb wire looking tattoo going around one ankle. Who knew what she had elsewhere on her body. Her overall appearance, not including the expensive dress, was that of someone who grew up on the street, the hard way.

I believe the only reason Angie Wilson allowed us to enter her home was to show it off. They lived in a very large home in Château Estates in Kenner, near the New Orleans International Airport. Her home was probably close to four thousand square feet. It was one of those homes with a twenty-foot ceiling in the center of an open floor plan. At the entry was a large canvas painted by a popular local artist. It was of a double shotgun house, like I lived in, that distorted the angle and focus of the building so it appeared to be looming out at you. From the front door, you could see straight back to a wall of windows that showed a beautiful landscaped patio, pool and a very large yard. Angie Wilson was doing her best to spend the money her husband made. That was where the niceness ended.

Her furniture had a warehouse outlet look about it compared to the family heirlooms and coordinated décor that tastefully appointed Esme's home.

Jiff did all the talking. He introduced us and told Angie we were retained or hired by the family of Ian and Sophie Saucier to look into their deaths. He skipped telling her he represented Phillip.

"I know what retained means. What do you want?" she finally asked us after we were inside.

She did not offer us to take a seat nor did she offer us anything to drink—a courtesy southerners, and especially New Orleanians, extend those they invite or allow into their homes. In short, she had no manners.

"Angie, don't you remember me? I came to your wedding with Phillip. I've known Ian and Phillip since high school," Jiff said pulling out his charm.

"I remember you," she said to Jiff, then she looked me up and down.

Jiff took this to mean he needed to introduce me. "This is Brandy Alexander. We're colleagues at my firm, and I'm trying to help figure out when happened to Ian and Sophie," he said.

"Are you with the police?" she snapped. "If not, you ought to stay out of it."

"We're not with the police, but right now, the only suspects the police have, who they will be looking at closely, are Phillip and you. You both were partners with the Sauciers in the fireworks business. You know the police. They will look to find suspects close to home first," Jiff said with a heartfelt delivery as if her well-being was his only concern.

"So?" she asked indignant that Jiff even suggested it.

"Well, I understand you and Phillip took out a life insurance policy on Ian and Sophie. The insurance company contacted me since I am Ian's attorney of record," Jiff said.

"That's none of your business whether I made a claim. That's money I'm entitled to, and I think you better leave, now," she said walking the few steps to the entry and opening the door indicating it was our time to exit.

Oh boy, Angie was dumb as a rock.

Once in Jiff's car I said, "Well, now we know she made a claim on the life insurance money and I bet Phillip doesn't know it yet. Funny, she never said we, but rather I, as in for herself."

"I wish I could be a fly on the wall when Hanky and Taylor interrogate her," Jiff said.

"Speaking of which, it might be time to pay some good will forward," I said and made a call to Detective Taylor's cell phone.

"Hello Miss Alexander," he answered. "Didn't we just see each other outside of criminal court after your wedding?"

"Yes, we did run into each other outside of the courthouse."

"I was sitting here waiting for your call to see how I can further assist you today. Do you need me to help plan your honeymoon? I hear Hawaii is very romantic. If the two of you are more of an adventure seeking couple, I'd recommend scuba diving in Hawaii—best of both worlds," he said, and I could just imagine the smile on his face he was having at my expense.

Ignoring his last comment, I said, "Detective, how nice of you. I'm calling to give you some info you may or may not find helpful. We talked to Angie Wilson, who is not very friendly by the way, even though Jiff has known her for years and went to her wedding. You might want to bring a Taser with you if you are going to try to question her. Angie Wilson confirmed she knew about the million-dollar life insurance policy on Ian, Sophie Saucier and her husband."

"You don't say?" Taylor said trying not to give away the fact he probably didn't know or if he did, he didn't want to share the information he had.

"Well, I think she filed a claim already. Her exact words escape me, but it was something like it wasn't any of our business if she already made a claim. Angie Wilson could really be in the pink if something happens to her husband. Don't those policies usually pay double for accidental deaths?" I asked.

"Well, Miss Alexander, thank you for calling with that information," he said.

"You didn't happen to have the coroner's report on your desk when you got back to your office, did you? The report that IDs the bodies in the house fire?" I asked.

"No, no report, but I will get back to you on that. But, let me ask you, do you know if Ian Saucier or his wife had a motorcycle or a friend with one? There were tire tracks that looked to belong to a motorcycle going over the levee from their backyard which looked kinda fresh that night," he said.

"Motorcycle? I'll ask Jiff and get back to you if Sophie or Ian owned one," I said. "A motorcycle, huh. Did forensics ID it from the tire tracks to tell what kind it is?"

"Where did you say you two were going on your honeymoon?" Detective Taylor asked me.

"I'll take that as a yes on the forensics and I'll wait to hear from you unless I have some other information I come across you should know," I said and then I hung up.

"Remind me never to tick you off," Jiff said. "You turned up the heat on old Angie mentioning the double indemnity on accidents...just in case Taylor didn't think of it."

"Oh, he thought of it. I just wanted him to know we thought of it too," I said. "Where are we on all of this?" I asked. "Angie Wilson is despicable. What did a nice guy like Phillip ever see in her? I can't see how he dated her, let alone married her?"

Jiff looked like he was about to answer, and I more or less knew what she wrangled Phillip with, so I hurriedly added, "Never mind. From those tats on her, I'm sure she knows a lot of...ways to keep ol' Phillip entertained."

We drove in silence for a few minutes.

"Are you hungry?" Jiff asked.

"A little. Let's go somewhere for a drink and a quick bite," I said.

"No, we're going somewhere nice to eat and relax," Jiff said picking up his phone and calling Ralph's On the Park to confirm a reservation he had already made at some earlier time today. "We've been jumping from one interview to the next usually during the dinner hour. I need a civilized dinner with waiters and someone else who clears the table."

"That's only happened two days in a row, counting today," I said.

"It has only been two days? It feels like we've been at this grind for weeks. What do you say to Ralph's On the Park?" he asked.

I nodded my okay with the dinner plans. What? Another three squares a day man. Men only think of food.

Ralph's was on City Park Avenue. The dining room had windowed walls that provided a lovely view of the park's majestic oak trees from every table. Once the valet opened my door, Jiff ushered me into the bar area first. I always like having a drink at the bar, and in this case, it's a grand U-shaped bar with a copper counter-top so you can see everyone sitting around it. There are a few tables around the perimeter but sitting at the bar is way more fun. The patrons and bartenders are a congenial crowd and usually bond in conversation over a current event. The topic today was last week's rainstorm that flooded most of mid-city businesses. It was a break from the ever popular, and never ending, discussion on how the Saints were robbed of going to the Super Bowl via the bad referee call.

From our seats I had a view of the park across the street and the dueling oaks under which many an insult was solved back in the day. The thought of men dueling for honor or to save face inspired me to order a signature cocktail.

"I'll have a Death in the Oaks," I told the bartender when he came over to take our order. When he returned with our drinks, he slid a bar napkin in front of us and placed my drink, a champagne drink with pomegranate, a cucumber slice, absinthe and cane sugar on it. Jiff had an Oak Fashioned—a drink that's my dad's favorite—in a City Park oak smoked glass with bourbon, a Luxardo Cherry garnished with an orange slice.

There was a bar menu we could have snacked on but we both liked sitting at the bar having a cocktail to unwind by. For me, the stop at the bar started distancing the events of the day so I could have a fresh look at them later. We were planning to move to a table for dinner to exchange thoughts about matters at hand. Tonight, I wondered if we'd discuss the case we were trying to solve or our wedding plans.

The maître d' came by and said our table was ready whenever we were. We were halfway through our cocktail so he had a waiter carry them on a tray to our table for us. We were sitting at a window with a clear view of an entrance to the park with one of the original wrought iron arches that had the CITY PARK name inscribed on it. The dining room tables were about half full of dinner patrons so it was quiet and calm. I was glad for a peaceful evening.

We sat enjoying our cocktails and looking over the menu. I selected a Crawfish Daniel salad and Jiff ordered the Crawfish Pasta. He pointed to a bottle on the Wine Menu for the waiter to bring us. I didn't see what he ordered but he always ordered something I liked.

"I like this place," Jiff said. "It feels comfortable but classy, you know what I mean?"

"Yes, I think so, too," I said, looking out the windows at the majestic oaks that had been standing there providing romantic picnic spots or terrifying dueling locations for over three hundred years. They were graceful, stoic and resilient even after all the hurricanes and storms that visited them.

When I looked back to the table, there was a small jewelry box set in front of me with a smiling Jiff sitting behind it, watching me intently.

"Will you marry me?" Jiff asked.

"I think you already asked me and Meaux that question. We both said yes."

"I did, but not formally. Besides, I like hearing your answer. This is the formal version complete with the engagement ring," he said opening the box, removing the ring to put on my hand. It was a stunning, very large and exquisite emerald-cut diamond.

It took my breath away it was so beautiful. It felt like I stared at that ring an hour before I realized I owed Jiff an answer.

"Yes. Again," I said. "I will marry you, and so will Meaux."

As Jiff slid the ring on my finger, I heard a pop and the waiter came over with a bottle of champagne for us. It was Dom Pérignon. Our waiter showed the bottle to Jiff who nodded his approval. He then poured us each a flute while a busboy appeared with an ice bucket to set up at the end of our table.

"This fits perfectly," I said. "How did you do that, know my ring finger size? I don't think I even know it."

"I measured your finger with a piece of string while you were sleeping, and I borrowed one of the rings I see you wear from time to time and brought them to the jeweler," he said beaming from ear to ear.

"It's going to be hard to keep our engagement a secret if I am wearing this rock. I might even need assistance to lift my hand to show people if they ask to see my ring," I said. The diamond was in a sophisticated, stunning gold setting.

"You can have the setting changed to anything you want," he said.

"I wouldn't change a thing," I said admiring it on my hand.

"That is the diamond my grandfather gave to my grandmother. She wanted you to have it, and suggested a plain setting so I could add more diamonds to it in the wedding band," he said smiling from ear to ear.

"Jiff, I don't need more diamonds. It means a lot to me that your grandmother wanted me to have her ring. This makes it a family heirloom. I am thrilled to have it, but I don't want us to get lost in the wedding thing the way I've seen so many couples do," I said. "I don't want it to become such a stressful ordeal for the two of us that we ever have a moment where we're sorry we decided to get married."

"I want you to have whatever you want, big wedding, small wedding, anything," he said.

"Well, what I want is for it to be special for the two of us. You mentioned looking for a house together. This is a lot to take on with the work we both do. Both of us have demands that sometimes require us to work longer hours or weekends. How are we supposed to plan a wedding and buy a house with our schedules?"

"They're called wedding planners?" he asked in a mocking question. "Even I know that."

I just looked at him.

"If it's the money, don't worry about that," he said.

"No, it's not that, although a wedding and a wedding planner could seriously impact my savings, not to mention my share of the down payment I'll have to put up for our house," I said. "You know my family is supposed to pay for the wedding, but you know the relationship I have with my mother. I don't plan on asking my parents to pay for anything. Remember, she tried to pawn me off marrying Dante, something he's never asked me, by the way, piggybacking onto my sister's shotgun fiasco so she wouldn't have to pay for me at a later date."

The thought of that ordeal brought me to tears. I took stock of myself and decided I wasn't going to let my mother ruin this wonderful evening with my wonderful guy as I dabbed them away.

Jiff took both my hands in his. "I know you have issues with your mother, but my mother will help with anything you need, planning or getting things done."

"I wish your mother would adopt me," I said smiling.

"How would that look? You and I getting married if we're brother and sister?"

"All of you are adopted, so we wouldn't be related, not that it would matter," I said. "We live in the south where people marry their brothers or sisters, aunts or uncles all the time."

"You know people would find that odd, right?" Jiff asked, very amused by it all.

I let out a heavy sigh and had to admit, "You're

right. I was just trying to keep my mind off my mother and how that will probably go when I work up the courage to tell her."

"My mother and the wives or girlfriends of my brothers will all help. You don't have to overwhelm yourself. Give them all a task you need help with, and it will get done," Jiff said smiling.

"I know they will all help if we ask, and I appreciate it," I said. "We will probably need their help even if we make the plans and keep it small, although two hundred people is not small. The more people involved means it takes our attention away from where it belongs, and that's on you and I. So, let's keep the ceremony small."

"Small? That will be impossible with just the size of my family," he said.

"I want our families there...well, I want your family there at any rate. I don't want the big, traditional wedding like our parents had because I don't want to turn into Bridezilla. I get weak in the knees thinking of finding a church date, hiring limousines, florists, a wedding dress, bridesmaids' dresses, bridal showers, registries to picking out this and that, or asking one friend over another to be bridesmaids, which will get blown out of control with just your family. If I have to find a bridesmaid for each of your brothers, then we have an army of a wedding party," I said. I thought he looked disappointed. I added, "I hope I'm not hurting your feelings."

"Are you kidding? Most men would like to keep it down to three people, the bride, the groom and whoever officiates," he said laughing.

"While you are nothing like most men, I like the idea of keeping it to three, but I think we still need witnesses," I said, taking a sip of champagne. "That could bump the crowd up to five or six people. See how fast these things get out of control?"

"Five or six? That's outrageous, but I'll go along with whatever you want," he said rubbing both of my hands between his.

I moved my hand with the engagement ring on top of one of his saying, "I want to look at it some more. What if, and I'm just throwing out ideas here, we send out invitations to come to a party? We say we're going to make an announcement. Everyone will think we're announcing our engagement, but the announcement is we're married. We can have a small ceremony in a church, or at your dad's building you mentioned, then follow it with the party that everyone is invited to. We can celebrate with friends and family, but our wedding will be special for us, not the twenty or thirty people we would have to have with groomsmen, ushers, flower girls, bridesmaids, ring bearers, someone to play music, florists, caterers, cake makers, and I can't even think of who or what else."

"Well...when you list them all...I'm kinda liking

your idea more and more," he said as his eyes glazed over, looking like the groom who just realized what he was getting into.

"Let's think in terms of that idea for a few days and if you are still in agreement, or you want something else, then we can talk about it," I said.

"My dad owns a building in the French Quarter where we've always held our family receptions and special events there. It's really quite nice. It was a French Quarter home that took up about a quarter of a block we renovated and rent for meetings, parties or special events. It will accommodate from five or six," he said smiling, "up to two hundred people."

"Well, that would be great," I said. "Finding a place or a church tends to dictate the date of the event. You will need to find out when it's available."

"I do like the idea of keeping the chaos to a minimum. Getting married and then announcing it at a celebratory party sounds better the more I think about it. We need to think about when we want to get married. I want to make sure we have my dad's building, even if we have to cancel someone's reservation," he said kissing my hand.

"Why don't you find out when it's not reserved and we'll pick one of those dates?" I asked.

"See, I knew you were the smart one," he said squeezing my hand. "I want to sit here, enjoy our champagne, and look at you."

Chapter Nine

Thursday a.m.

THURSDAY WAS A perfectly delightful day in New Orleans. The temperature was in the 90's, but the humidity was very low, making for a very pleasant summer day. I was in a glorious mood driving to work until the phone rang and without looking at the caller ID, I answered it with a song in my heart and a smile on my face, "Hello, Brandy speaking!"

On the other end of the line Dante's all too familiar voice came through asking, "Brandy, Hanky said you got married. Is that true?"

I almost dropped the phone. I was in too good a mood to let this mess me up, but it did fluster me. A lot. I had to think fast. I did not want to lie to him. I decided to answer in truths. I said, "Hanky heard it because Hanky said it. Some detective she is. I'm not married. Hanky and Taylor saw Jiff and me at the criminal court building and asked me the same question. What's wrong with her?"

All of which was true and I felt I had dodged a freight train. It was time to change the subject, fast.

"I figured you weren't. I told her you'd tell me if you were," Dante said, and just like that my great mood made me feel like the biggest hypocrite. Suzanne was right. I had to tell him first before I made the big announcement.

"I would tell you before anyone else. I mean, I will," I tried to answer so I didn't sound like the biggest fake. "Is that why you called me?"

"Not just that. Taylor said you knew the victims in the house fire. We're trying to find their next of kin," Dante said. "It's been a week since the fire and the explosion."

"Victim. I only know of one victim in that fire. If there are more, I don't know them, but Jiff might," I said. "I was supposed to meet them the next day at a party they were having at the house that burned. I told you this already, the night of the fire."

"Do you know their next of kin?" he asked.

"Why do you keep asking like there's more than one victim? I'm telling you I only know of one victim who might have been in the house. What are you saying? Was there more than one person found in the fire?" I asked.

Dante exhaled loudly so I could hear how exasperated he was with me over the phone. When he realized

I wasn't going to give him what he wanted, he added, "Forensics shows two sets of DNA in cremated remains but not enough to identify them. The coroner thinks the two are someone's ashes left there on a mantle, in an urn or something. There was a third body found burned beyond recognition. The coroner is trying to make an ID from the DNA, but he doesn't have anything yet." Then he paused before he added, "So, can you give me the name of someone who might be the next of kin for these people? I don't want to call Heinkel unless I have to."

There it was. Big bad Dante didn't want to call my boyfriend and ask him something. So, I decided to help him out. "It's probably Sophie Saucier," I said feeling lower than I did minutes ago after not telling Dante the whole truth and nothing but the truth concerning my engagement status.

"It's not Sophie Saucier. It's not any female for that matter. Coroner says it's definitely a male from the DNA markers. Do you know if she had a brother?" he asked.

Maybe Ian had a brother that was there, I had no idea, so I gave Dante the contact info for Sophie's sister, Esme Bourgeois. Now, I knew it wasn't Sophie in the fire, but who was the male person and where was Sophie?

"Do you know about the life insurance policies that

Ian Saucier and his partner, Phillip Wilson, took out on each other just a couple of weeks ago?" I asked him.

"Yes," he said.

"Don't the insurance companies pay double for accidental deaths?" I asked.

"I believe they do," Dante answered a little slowly so it made me think this fact just dawned on him.

"And since the policy was a million-dollar policy, wife Angie and her husband Phillip will make out like bandits. Imagine if something happens to Phillip? Then Angie would make six million dollars with three policy payouts," I said. "That makes me think there's more to this fire and explosion than bad luck."

"You could be right," he said and hung up. I was going to try to gently mention that Jiff and I were planning our future together, but Hanky might have done me a favor by planting the seed for me.

Hanging up without saying goodbye was Dante's signature move. He has done this his entire life. While I know to expect it, it still bugs me.

I couldn't wait to tell Jiff about it not being Sophie in the fire, but the call went to voicemail. He was likely in court. I texted him and left a message saying that there was a body, a male, found at Ian and Sophie's house, along with two other sets of DNA the coroner thought might be cremated remains. Jiff texted me back a few minutes later and said the two DNAs are likely

Ian's parents who were in urns on the mantle in the living room over the fireplace.

I was wondering if the person found could have been Ian, but he was supposed to be on the barge. Could he have left the barge and come back home? Did Ian or Sophie have a brother? If it was Ian, where was Sophie?

The parking gate to the building I worked in opened after I punched in my security code the second time. I was very distracted from Dante's phone call. It was going to be tough telling him I was planning to marry Jiff. I didn't want to do it on the phone and something made me feel like Hanky had set him up to ambush me. Hanky was always on Dante's side.

The day was uneventful, but I kept busy going on appointments with clients, meeting them out of my office. This always made my day fly by and I enjoyed meeting the clients and hearing their problems— problems I could solve.

After my morning appointments ended right before lunch, I called Jiff's cell phone and found him at his office. I wanted to know if anything new came up regarding Phillip, Ian, and Sophie.

I said to Jiff, "Hey, are you free for lunch? I wanted to talk about what we know, or think we know, with the Ian and Sophie situation. Something doesn't feel right about any of it."

"Can't do lunch, I'm slammed," he said.

"Well, I can grab a rolling lunch," I said. "I've got afternoon appointments."

"What doesn't feel right in particular?" he asked.

"I find it odd that it's a male identified in the fire, according to Dante. So, where is Sophie? Ian hasn't turned up—dead or alive—could it be him? Also, no one has said anything about Sophie's car, or Ian's car for that matter. I didn't see a car in the drive or garage the night of the fire."

"It could be at the boathouse where Ian met Freddie," Jiff said. "No telling where Sophie's car is. Maybe at their office. We need to ask Phillip."

"It seems Phillip might have mentioned it if Ian's car was still at the office. I'll call Esme. We need to ask her if Sophie stopped by with anyone, or if she had her car, or rode with someone when she dropped Blast off on the day of the fire," I said.

"Yes, there might be a simple explanation, like the fire department moved it for better access and to try to save the vehicle when they got there," Jiff said.

"I don't think so. Have you ever seen what they do to a vehicle in their way? They just hook it and drag it up the street. You can find it by following the rubber tire marks left by the locked brakes," I said. "They should leave coupons on the windshield of the cars they tow from brake repair shops."

Jiff tilted his head to give me his 'what else' look.

"It feels off that Ian was waiting to speak with you at the party but first he wrote and mailed a letter to you a few days before. Why would he do that? Was it in case something went wrong? Or because he anticipated he and Phillip might be in danger? But Sophie? Did he feel she could be in danger too? Doesn't that seem weird to you?" I asked. "This is going to sound heartless, but neither one of them, or any part of them, has been found."

"Everything seems weird, wrong or off," he said. "Ian not being found is understandable. He was blown to bits and the water was rough that night so he could have been scattered and anything that was left would be consumed by marine life. Sophie, I have no idea what happened to her unless she was so badly cremated they can't find any DNA to identify her."

I was glad to hear him say it. I had been thinking it, but hearing it from someone is always a shock if the person or persons were close to you.

"We need to find out more about what has gone on with Ian and Phillip's work," I said.

"Well, we can't talk to the Director. He covered up the problems when Ian talked to him, according to Phillip," Jiff said. "He's in on it and hiding something."

"Well, maybe one of their co-workers might have something useful to add," I said. "Or, maybe a better idea is to do some research on those labs Phillip said never sent back the test results."

"I'll get Michelle, my investigator, on it," Jiff said.

Thursday after lunch

USUALLY I DON'T answer calls that come to my cell phone that aren't in my contact list. I let them leave a message. Lately, my situation with Jiff had me in more of a euphoric mood than usual and I wasn't making the same tried and true decisions. This time I answered, and I'm glad I did. "Hello," but I didn't give my name like I do for business calls.

"It's Phillip," he answered in a rush. "Brandy? Is this you?"

"Yes. What's up, Phillip? Do you need to reach Jiff?"

"Yeah, I want to talk to him and soon. I think someone is following me," he said.

"Where are you now?"

"At my office. There was a car following me to work, and now it's parked across the street like they are waiting for me to leave," he said.

"Can you see who's in the car or get the license plate?" I asked.

"Not without letting them know I see them. The car is an Escalade with blacked out windows. I can't see inside," he said. "I don't know if it's one or two people in it."

Phillip sounded distracted.

"Sit tight. I'll get in touch with Jiff or his office and see if one of his investigators is around to drive over there. I'll call you back. What number is this?" I asked.

"This is one of the disposable phones we keep for the temp guys we hire who don't have cell phones. If we don't get them back after the team uses them, we turn them off and someone else has to pay to re-activate them. They're disposable mostly. No one's used this one before, so I thought it would be safe to call you on."

Oh boy. Phillip now had me rattled.

"I'll call you back on this number in a couple of minutes," I said. I immediately called Jiff and it went to voicemail, and then he sent me a text saying he was in court. I called his office and asked the receptionist who was Jiff's backup, and she transferred me through to one of his brothers.

After speaking to Jiff's brother and telling him the basics, he said he'd go pick up Phillip with one of his investigators and bring him back to the office. I gave him Phillip's burner phone number and said "I'll call him back and let him know the plan, otherwise, I don't think he's going to answer the phone. And, I'm coming with you so do you want to pick me up or I'll drive over to your office?"

"I'll pick you up. You're on Poydras and it's on the way," he said.

I called Phillip and told him Jiff's brother, Jay, is going to pick him up, and I'll be with him. "Get ready, we will pull up in front. I'll call you after the other car leaves and you come out and get in. I don't know what car I'll be in. I'll tell you when I call back after we're there," I said.

Phillip asks, "How do you know the car will leave?"

"We're coming in two cars. I'll be in the one that waits while the other one pulls up behind the Escalade and gets the license plate. They will get out holding up a badge. It's an auxiliary police department badge, but it's an official badge. The Escalade will leave. That car will follow them. I will call you first and let you know when we are pulling up in the second car the Escalade will not see. If they don't leave, Jiff's brother will call the police, but the Escalade will never see or know it's you. They might have cloned your cell phone so they knew when you were moving and who you are calling," I said. "Leave it at your office when you come out. Lock it in a desk or somewhere no one will find it."

After Jay picked me up, I noticed a white van following us. When I looked over my shoulder, Jay said, "The ever present and hard to track, white van. They'll be in a black car—that makes them the bad guy. Our guys will be in a white car—that makes us the good guys."

His quick wit and smiling face took the edge off of the situation for me. He was pleasant and engaging. We had met at a family gathering where I was first introduced to the entire Heinkel family.

Jay looked a lot like Jiff tall, fit and attractive with dark hair and dark eyes. His demeanor was less business than Jiff and a lot more casual. He was approachable with a knack to make you smile and put you at ease. Of course, Jiff might be like that also when someone first meets him. Our first meeting was in the middle of St. Charles Avenue at Lee Circle during a Mardi Gras parade where we kissed before we knew each other's name. I'd have to say that definitely made Jiff approachable.

"Do you think they'll get the license plate before the vehicle leaves?" I asked.

"Yes, but the car will likely be stolen. We'll run it anyway. Never know, we might get lucky," he said.

Jay had a two-way radio, and when we got close the Phillip's office, he told the driver of the white van we were pulling over to wait. The van driver pulled up behind the Escalade and a man on the passenger side, in what looked like all black SWAT cargo pants and a shirt, showing a shiny official-looking shield on his belt, got out and started walking toward the Escalade. The Escalade took off. A static-y voice came over the radio giving Jay the all clear for us to approach the building. I called Phillip and told him we were in a dark blue

Mercedes pulling up in front in about fifteen seconds.

A nervous looking Phillip came darting out the front door, stopped, looked around and then realized he had to lock the front door. He did while checking over his shoulder. Jay got out of the car and opened a rear passenger door for him, saying he was going to take him back to Jiff's office.

"Thanks, Brandy, for getting me out of there. I've always had nerves of steel, but after what happened to Ian and Sophie, I didn't want to take any chances," Phillip said.

After I introduced Jiff's brother, Jay asked, "So what do you do to have nerves of steel?"

"I was in the military, Afghanistan, with EOD. Explosive Ordinance Disposal," he said.

"Oh-h-h. I guess it does take a bit to rattle you," Jay said checking Phillip out in the rearview mirror.

Jay parked in a section of the garage where card access was required. This was the second card swipe required to get into the security gated parking section for about twenty cars in Canal Place close to a bank of elevators. These elevators, he explained, were private or he called them escape elevators for the tenants in Canal Place, many of whom were lawyers and might want to avoid a hostile client who just drops by. The same card that granted us access to the secure parking area also worked in the elevator allowing us to punch in the floor we wished to reach.

"So this is the Bat Cave entrance?" I asked. "Jiff has never taken me this way…I wonder why?"

"We rarely use it unless we are taking someone in or out of the office and we don't want to draw attention to them, like now. We use this entrance and exit when we're trying to avoid the press or a volatile individual," he said.

"I feel so special," I said by way of trying to joke.

It was late in the day, almost 4:30 p.m. and a lot of people would be leaving through the main lobby so it was a good thing we used this way in. Jay showed Phillip and I into Jiff's conference room adjacent to his office. The room could seat about six to eight people comfortably.

All of the partners' offices had these conference rooms varying in size. Jiff's dad had the largest one and his brothers had rooms to accommodate different size groups. The furniture in Jiff's office, including his conference room, was made out of sandalwood. It still had a nice, clean aroma when you walked into either room like you're entering a spa. It caused you to relax immediately. After the first time I was in his office and mentioned it, he said he picked it because the fragrance could last decades. He had said once he selected it, it was decided everyone's office would be sandalwood. The offices always smelled good when you stepped off the elevators.

I made a call to Suzanne to let her know I'd be

running late and I asked her to let the dogs out and feed them before she left for work. She agreed as always.

Phil and I waited in Jiff's conference room for him to get back from court. While we were waiting, Michelle, Jiff's investigator, came in with news on the labs.

"It's not good," she said. "They've been cited in the past for numerous offenses and fines. Then, three years ago...voila...no more fines. Why?"

"Didn't you and Ian start working there about three years ago?" I asked Phillip.

"Yes, and we were hired at the same time Angie's dad was promoted to the position he has now. I'm sure that's why he hired us," Phillip said.

"Well, let me go look into Angie's dad. What's his name and address?" she asked.

Phillip gave it to her and she left to go dig up anything she could find on him. I followed her out, asking her where the ladies room was. Once in the hallway and out of earshot from Phillip, I followed Michelle and said, "I know you have to clear this with Jiff, but could you do a background check on Angie, his wife?" nodding in the direction of Phillip sitting in the conference room.

"Yeah. Maiden name same as the dad's, I'm guessing," Michelle said jotting down a note. "Know of any other names, aliases she or the dad used?"

"Not that I know of, and I think her maiden name is the same as the dad's, but who knows. She lives in Kenner now, in a big house in Château Estates," I said. "Oh, and her brother. Phillip refers to his wife's brother—his brother-in-law—as a freak-a-zoid, which isn't a clinical name for how weird he is, but I guess it should be."

"I know the type," Michelle said laughing. "What's his name? The freak-a-zoid?"

"Freddie. Freddie the Freak-a-zoid," I said. "Too bad that's not his real name or his alias, although it fits. His real name is Freddie Finklestein, Jr. He does have a street name or alias he goes by and a rap sheet, I guess. Phillip said Freddie ran in a biker gang in his misguided youth. Since I'm only familiar with one biker gang, the Hell's Angels, maybe he was part of the local chapter. He went by the nickname of Coke Bottle Freddie. I've been told he still wears very thick eyeglasses."

"Kids can be so cruel," Michelle said. "Although some don't ever get the name they truly deserve, if you know what I mean."

"Yeah. Phillip told Jiff that even Freddie's teachers in school called him Coke Bottle Freddie," I said.

"Aww, now that's bad. I almost feel sorry for him," Michelle said.

"Don't. He's a freak-a-zoid with or without thick glasses," I said.

Chapter Ten

Thursday p.m.

J IFF RETURNED TO his office around 4:45 p.m. while I was speaking with Michelle. She left when he walked up to us in the hall.

"Thanks for calling Jay and helping with Phillip," he said. "The hearing lasted a lot longer than I anticipated or I would have been back sooner."

"No problem," I said as he brushed an errant hair away from my face, then leaned in kissing my forehead. "Phillip is in the conference room next to your office."

Phillip jumped to his feet when Jiff and I entered the conference room while he reached to shake Jiff's hand.

"Phillip had quite an encounter. There was a black Escalade parked outside his office that took off when your guys pulled up behind it," I said.

"Try to relax, Phil," Jiff said. "We'll figure this out."

"I think whoever killed Ian and Sophie is now after

me," Phillip said. "I gotta think it's Angie's uncle. If she knew we were starting a lab, then her dad knew and probably told him."

"We can't dismiss the possibility, so we will see if we can verify it, but first we need to keep you safe," Jiff said. "Can you take a couple of days off without raising suspicion from Angie or the EPA?"

"Maybe. Why?" Phillip asked pacing in the conference room.

"I want you in a place no one knows where you are until we finish the background investigation," Jiff said. "It's a precaution, but one I think we should take since this incident has you rattled."

"I could say I'm going on a deep-sea fishing trip. Some of the guys Ian and I served with have been talking about planning a trip like that for a few months. I have some vacation days, and Angie will not want to follow me on that," Phillip said.

"Good. Text her and your job. This is Thursday, so tell them you are taking a long weekend and will be back on Tuesday. Tell Angie you'll be out on a fishing boat for three or four days. Tell her you'll call her when you're back in range, if you have a signal. Tell your office you're just taking some time off unless they make you take vacation days. Don't give them specifics," Jiff said. "If they ask, be brief. Say you're going to visit friends. That's it."

"Okay. While I was waiting for you, I thought of someone you should talk to that Ian and I worked with. Ed Chauvin is an environmentalist, older guy, close to retirement but Ian and I trust him. Ed told us he used to go fishing with his dad in this area when he was a kid. He's taken photos over the years and you can see how the area changed from year to year as Ed and his dad grew older in the pictures. The guy has forty plus years of photos documenting the decline in the area.

"Ed worked with us collecting samples. Ian asked Ed if his samples ever came back as toxic from a particular area. Ed pulled us aside and said we needed to go somewhere to have lunch and then he'd talk about it. We grabbed some sandwiches and ate outside at a picnic table in a nearby park. He said he would send in samples from an area he's watched decline since he was a kid to see what's going on in there. He marked those samples as coming from an area he was working in. Even those samples came back cleaned." He has photos of two areas we've taken samples from over the last forty to fifty years. One continues to decline while the other is barely recovering with minimum vegetation regrowth. Ed has photos of two headed turtles, and some very weird fish. It's a visual documentary of the devastation done to that area over the last three decades."

Jiff said, "If they were mandated to stop fracking or

searching for oil, by now the damage should not be increasing. It should be decreasing unless they lied or they are still doing something illegal."

"Somebody is lying," Phillip said, "and my money is on Angie's uncle."

Jiff called Michelle into the meeting and asked Phillip to give her the names of the labs in question along with any other labs they use. Jiff also asked Phillip to give Michelle the full names of Angie, Angie's dad and her uncle, instructing Michelle to run investigative background checks on them.

"I started running a background check on Fred Finkelstein, Jr. already. You want me to keep doing that?" Michelle asked.

"Angie's brother," Phillip said by way of an answer to the question appearing on Jiff's face.

"I asked her," I said.

"Yes, him too," Jiff answered.

"What I already have on the brother, Freddie Jr, is he has direct deposits being made from his dad and uncle, weekly. He owns a new motorcycle he doesn't owe money on and he lives with another guy who has a lot of drug arrests. I'll check the dad and uncle and see if I can find any deposits made to them from one of those labs," Michelle said standing up to leave. "I'll search any deposits or money given to them in addition to their paychecks."

Jiff nodded for her to get started.

"Sounds like Freddie. Still trying to hang out with the rough guys," Phillip said as Michelle left the room.

"Anything else you can think of that Ian or Sophie said or did before the 4th that was out of the ordinary?" Jiff asked.

"No, not really. This is all a constant blur when I try to remember anything," Phillip said.

"Okay, let's reconvene when Michelle has something on the labs, and Angie or her relatives," Jiff said.

Phillip stood to leave, and Jiff gave him the keys to his condo on the lake.

"Take these and stay at my place for a day or so if you are worried about someone following you. We're about the same size. I have lots of casual wear, T-shirts, shorts, long pants and dress shirts. Use whatever you need," Jiff said.

"Man, I don't want to put you out," Phillip said.

"I'll stay at Brandy's. You can have the place to yourself. Felix is our driver and he'll take you out the back way…"

"The Bat Cave entrance," I said as a matter of informing Phillip in case he forgot.

Jiff looked at me and said, "That's what I always thought of it as, just never said it out loud." Then, to Phillip he said, "Felix will drop you at my condo and then he will go to your office to get anything you need.

Leave your car right where it is. If Angie asks if you need a ride, say one of your friends will pick you up. Turn your phone off and leave it on my desk."

"I told him to leave it in his office. Do you want Felix to get it?" I said.

"No. That's fine where it is. Here's a burner phone. If you need to go somewhere, which I strongly urge you not to do, call the office here and Felix will come get you. If you need something, anything, lunch, food, something from your office, you can trust Felix like you trust us. Call here and ask him to get it for you. Felix is very good at not being followed. Do not leave to go anywhere unless Felix takes you."

When Felix came in to escort Phillip out, I noticed he was the tall Chinese man who was the driver of the white van used to intimidate the Escalade while I rode with Jay.

Jiff instructed Felix to take Phillip out the back way and try to go unnoticed. Phillip left with Felix.

"Why haven't you ever brought me in via the Bat Cave elevator? Jay brought us in that way with Phillip."

"That entrance is for those who we don't want anyone to see coming or going from here. You, I want the world to see me coming and going with you," he said smiling.

"Aww, that's so sweet," I said. "Also, why have I never met Felix before?"

Felix works for the firm. Dad met him and hired him years ago. Sometimes, we have high profile cases we feel justifies having a body guard, like this one. My dad hired him almost thirty years ago and uses him as a driver when he isn't... how shall we say it...escorting us. Felix was a prodigy and at fifteen taught Marshall Arts to the Chinese Army."

"Defected?" I asked.

"Yep. He came here on a container ship, and found my dad. He asked if he would help him with his immigration issue. My dad, the defender of lost causes—as you well know since we are all adopted—got him citizenship and then helped to get other members of his family here. Felix is very loyal. He's also very good at being a bodyguard, so don't mess with him," Jiff said. "But you can mess with me."

"I realize it's Happy Hour, but we need a half time recap of the game," I said, tucking the Felix info away in my brain until I might need it...bodyguard, chauffeur, all around helpful guy.

"You know it really turns me on when you use sport analogies," he said coming around the desk toward me with a big smile on his face.

"Not now, and not here. We have work to do," I said smiling. I hoped Jiff would always have this fun-loving attraction to me. "I'm calling a time out to partake of Happy Hour, and we can start the clock once we get home. How's that sound?"

"Sounds like a good plan," he said giving me a kiss that was way too quick. "Let's go to the bar downstairs. It's not crowded at this time of day. We can get a drink and discuss this."

Nodding approval, I picked up the papers I had pulled out, packed them up and followed Jiff to the regular bank of elevators. We walked into the restaurant, a nice upscale steak house in Canal Place, and found the place deserted.

"Is it open?" I asked checking my watch. It was 5:25 p.m.—past the end of the workday.

"Oh yeah, it's open. It starts to fill up with the nine-to-five crowd after six o'clock," he said pulling a chair out for me at one end of the long, mahogany-carved bar. I saw the bartender come through the kitchen door, raise the part of the bar closest to the kitchen and walk down to serve us.

"Hello, Mr. Heinkel," he said. I noticed his name-tag said his name was Winston.

"Good evening, Winston," Jiff started to say, but Winston cut him off.

"I can't hear you, Mr. Heinkel, and I'd like to meet the pretty lady you're with, but you have to wear your antenna," he said picking up some red cocktail stirrers and handed us each two. I noticed he had put one red stirrer behind each of his ears.

We looked at each other as Winston smiled. I took two and put one behind each ear. It reminded me of my dad working in the garage. Dad always parked a pencil behind one of his ears in case he needed it to measure something he was cutting or working on. I took the two Winston held out to Jiff and placed them behind his ears, and then I asked Winston, "Can you hear us now?"

"I can, so what can I get you to drink?" he asked, coming in loud and clear. He placed a cocktail napkin in front of each of us.

Jiff looked confused but ordered a beer. He looked at me and I ordered a glass of Pinot Grigio. When Winston went off to get our drinks, he said, "What do you make of this?"

"It's a slow Thursday night in New Orleans. He needs something to keep us entertained. It's fun."

Our drinks came, and Winston made himself scarce while we talked.

I took the sheet with my notes out of my oversized purse that doubled as a briefcase. "Here's what I think we know and what we don't know. I made a list of what I could remember. Let's see what doesn't add up. Here's the list I typed up."

Jiff reached for the list while I added, "You know, it feels like Ian had a premonition or put together some unrelated facts suggesting something was going to happen. Think about it. Three facts keep nibbling at me. One, Ian sent you a note before your scheduled meet as if giving you the facts you might need in advance. Two, he talked to Phillip and got million-dollar insurance policies on all three of them. Three, something Esme said about Sophie dropping Blast off at her house instead of keeping him upstairs, like Esme says she always does, is colliding in my mind."

"I didn't think about Blast, but the first two have swirled around in my head too when I wasn't grieving for my friends," he said.

Jiff and I both looked over the following list I made:

-   House fire – Three remains found. No female, only a male DNA, and possibly they are the cremated remains of Ian's parents in an urn. No Sophie.
-   Barge explosion – no evidence of Ian found, no DNA, only a shoe.
-   Cars found, Sophie's a block away, Ian's car likely at boathouse—need to verify.
-   Labs-Angie's uncle forced EPA agents to use – Michelle's investigating.
-   Need to speak with Ed Chauvin, Phillip and Ian's colleague.
-   Angie, Angie's father, Angie's uncle might all be

working for EPA (bribes)-Michelle doing background checks.

- Freddie, Angie's brother and employee of Ian and Phillip's firm – Michelle doing background checks.

- Motorcycle tracks seen night of the fire at Saucier home in lawn at back of house. Freddie's?

- Jack heard and saw someone (we don't know who other than a friend of Freddie's) pick Freddie up on a brand new Harley at Ian's boathouse before the explosion.

- Ian's computer, where is it?

"If Freddie brought Ian to the barge, what was the plan to come get him? We need to talk to Freddie. I'll see if Phillip can locate him for us," Jiff said.

"I'll call Dante to see if we can get any info from Ian's security cameras or computer. I want to ask him why was Sophie's car parked a block away from her house." I said. "It's late and I need to get home to see my Meaux. I'm sure you're hungry too," I said smiling.

"This is a great list. You might just be a better investigator then Michelle," he said reading the list.

"I sincerely doubt that. Michelle can find water in the desert," I said.

Just then a small group of five people that looked to

be office workers came in and sat at the distant end of the bar. Winston came out and greeted them, handing each two red cocktail stirrers which they all put on after looking at each other wondering if it was a trick. Soon, they were all ordering and talking with their antenna on.

A man came into the bar and headed in our direction. I recognized him as a judge I had met with Jiff one night at a party. The good thing about judges is you don't have to remember their names. You can just say, 'Hello, Judge'. He stopped next to Jiff and clapped him on the shoulder with one hand and extended his other for Jiff to shake.

I intervened and said, "Hello, Judge. You don't have on your antenna, so Jiff can't hear you." I reached across the bar and picked up two red stirrers and handed them to him. The judge saw where ours were placed and immediately put them behind his ears.

"Better?" he asked. "Just another crazy night in here, I see." Jiff and the judge exchanged a few words, and he was about to head off to a table where some others were being seated, but not before he grabbed a handful of red stirrers. "I think we'll need these if we want to order," he said.

As the restaurant area filled up, I noticed the waiter was handing patrons red stirrers and indicating how they needed to be worn as he pointed to his own head.

"Are you hungry? Do you want to eat here?" Jiff asked as he looked around.

"No, we can grab something on the way home. Our work here is done. We were the early adapters of the antenna movement and now it is a craze," I said.

"I don't know that I'd call it a craze," he said and paid our bill. "It's more like another weird blip on the New Orleans radar."

"Yes, but we were here when the blip happened!" I said as I followed him out.

JIFF WAS DRIVING us to my house when he said, "I'll call and have something delivered, or we can pick it up on the way home."

"That's a great idea if you want to stop and pick up Dixie Chicken," I said. "She makes the best fried chicken and potato salad, ever."

"Deal. You order and I'll run in and get it," he said. "Get me the same thing."

After getting dinner squared away, we drove in silence a few more minutes before he pulled up in front of Dixie Chicken in Lakeview. When Jiff jumped out of the car, I made a call to Dante's office and he picked up.

"Oh, you're working late," I said. "I thought I was going to leave you a message."

"You've got the real deal, so don't waste it...go," he

said.

"I just found out that Sophie Saucier, the woman whose house burned down, parked her car a block away. Has she been found yet? In the fire, or anywhere?" I asked.

"Maybe the Fire Department moved it," he said.

"I don't think so. It was a good block away," I said. "Why would a woman coming home the night before a big party park a block or two away from her home?"

There was silence.

"How can you be so sure the Fire Department didn't move it?" Dante asked.

"Because I've seen how they move cars, have you?" I asked. "Hers was found parked legally and not in the middle of the street. Also, there were no rubber tracks to it indicating it had been dragged up the street on the hook, which is how they typically move a vehicle. They are usually in a hurry to get it out of the way for the fire fighting vehicles. Those guys could never work for Triple A."

"Well, that does seem odd, and we still don't have a location on her yet," he said, "or an ID on the three remains we did find. Are you saying she should be listed as a missing person?"

"I don't know. That should be your call. You're the police. Hey, that reminds me. Did you get anything off of security cameras at their home? Maybe one of them will show Sophie parking her car," I said.

"No, that footage is toast, and no one else lives close enough to them on Lakeshore Drive to get a good shot of their house," Dante said. "I don't think Sophie Saucier was in the house. I don't think she went home."

"I don't think she did either. And, having nothing to go on—as in nothing found of Ian Saucier—maybe her husband wasn't blown to smithereens on that fireworks barge," I said. "But I do think someone was trying to kill them before you ask me why aren't they coming forward."

"Well, where are they?" Dante asked. "And why aren't they coming forward?"

I really thought my overly dramatic exhale to show my annoyance would get a response from him. Since it didn't, I said, "I don't know right this second, but let me check something and I'll get back to you." I heard Dante hang up before I could say goodbye.

When Jiff got back in the car and as we headed to my house, I said, "We need to get in touch with Ed Chauvin and then talk to Phillip and Esme together for some friendly information exchange."

Chapter Eleven

Thursday p.m.

I STARTED TO wonder, who were the labs Ian and Phillip were working for? Who were they sending bogus results on behalf of? What if Ian and Phillip turned whistleblower? This could get deadly serious real fast, more so than it had already. I believed it all had to connect, but how?

Jiff and I drove to my house, making plans to drive to Point à la Hache the next morning, a little tiny town southeast of New Orleans about three hours each way, to find Ed Chauvin, the guy Phillip and Ian worked with who had similar experiences with the lab. Jiff's cell phone rang. It was Chauvin saying Phillip gave him a head's up that we might be driving down to meet him. Ed thought it best if we didn't come down there poking around and asking questions. He was happy to send us the photos he had and write up a statement supporting the same experiences Ian and Phillip had when he sent his samples to the labs they were told to use. He told Jiff he'd call back over the weekend, after he sent the files of photos and documentation he had.

Ed said he would email the photos, lab results, and statements to us, but he couldn't do it until he was home for the weekend. He didn't trust the post office down there not to go through his mail and report to his boss. The postmaster was another one of Angie's relatives.

Jiff had put him on speakerphone and when the conversation with Ed was winding down, he told us he was putting his retirement paperwork in the next day. He asked Jiff to hold off calling and reporting this until after the weekend.

Wow, this was a huge time saver not having to drive halfway to Grand Isle. I saw my caller ID showed Anthony was calling.

As soon as I answered, he said, "I found the home-less guy, well, not found him, but saw him. I'm working right off France Road, and I heard a motorcy-cle go by and when I looked down from the roof, I saw him."

"How high up were you? Are you sure it was him?" I asked.

"Oh, I was hanging out of the fifth floor when I heard his bike. I just don't know where he came from or where he's squatting, but I'll keep an eye and an ear out for his bike. The sound is pretty distinct. I'll call you when I know for sure. Thought you'd want to know he's still around."

"Yes, thanks," I started to say, but Anthony had hung up.

"Who was that?" Jiff asked.

"Anthony. He said he saw the homeless guy on his motorcycle out in the east off France Road where he's working. Said he'd call back when he's got an idea where he might be crashing," I said.

"I'd say let's drive out there and take a look around, but that isn't the safest area and with all those warehouses and empty buildings, that guy could be parked in one and we'd never find him," he said. "Why don't we take a break from this for today? This works out for me since I want to go see the event manager of the building my dad owns so I can find out what dates are available for us to schedule our wedding."

"Good. I need to make some calls and run some errands myself, so take me back to my office and we'll catch up later this afternoon if that works for you," I said.

Back at my office I made some calls to clients and made sure nothing was on the verge of the explosions I witnessed with Jiff from the bow of his sailboat on the 4th of July. I felt there was nothing that needed my immediate attention, nor was there anyone around to take my calls. I decided to pay Frank, Julia's live-in assistant, a visit. Today was Julia's personal grooming day. She went for her weekly massage, manicure and pedicure so she wouldn't be around for at least three hours, and it would be safe to talk to Frank.

I walked up the brick sidewalk and steps to Julia's guest house. Frank had spotted me and opened the double doors by the time I got to the top step.

"Well, as I live and breathe," Frank said holding his arms out wide in anticipation of a big hug. He was wearing Capri pants, and a navy blue striped shirt like he was about to celebrate Bastille Day. The only thing missing was a beret. He did, however, have on enough mascara and eyeliner to look like one of the cast from *Les Misérable*.

"Frank, it's good to see you," I said. "It feels like I haven't been here in ages."

"That's because you haven't. C'mon in," he said.

"You look very French today, very ooh-la-la. What's up?" I asked after our big hug.

"Well...nothing really," he stopped and eyed me. "You look...very different yourself...happy," he said holding me at arm's length and giving me a once over with a skeptical look.

"I am. Thanks," I said.

"You know the Queen isn't in the tower drafting edicts to make my life more difficult," he said. "I'm afraid you missed her."

"This is when she goes for her nails, pedicure and whatever else she does at her weekly spa appointment, right?"

"Yes, that's why it's so tranquil and peaceful right now. So why are you here if you knew she wouldn't be?" Frank asked getting more suspicious. Frank loves a good secret or mystery to unravel especially if it means keeping Julia in the dark.

"Is there someplace we can go and talk...in private?" I asked.

"C'mon. We'll use the queen's bedchambers," he said and turned to climb the grand staircase. Every few steps he looked over his shoulder back at me with a look on his face that suggested he was trying to uncover the secret I wasn't telling him. Julia had her office on the second floor in an upstairs double parlor. On one side of the ten-foot pocket doors was her desk for hotel business and the other side—the one with the antique four-poster bed—for extra-curricular or monkey business.

The door was open and there were hats of every size, shape and color everywhere in her office/boudoir. Hats with lots of feathers, ribbons, and all kinds of weird strange stuff on them.

"What's with the hats?" I asked.

"She invited herself to a luncheon in a week or so for the hospitality industry. She thinks if she joins the local organization in the hotel market that will improve her standing in the city. That will last as long as she doesn't open her mouth...five minutes max," Frank said and turned to look at me. He put his hands on his hips and faced me. "Now what's going on?"

"Frank, you need to keep this a secret," I said. "Can you?"

"Are you getting married?" he asked.

"Yes, and that's what I want to talk to you about. I want to hire you to make my wedding dress," I said and watched as Frank jumped up and down clapping his hands together and making a joyful sound that was much like a pig squealing.

"I knew you looked extra happy," he said. "Of course, I'd be delighted to make your dress. How much time do we have? One minute..." he held up a finger. "Wait here, I'll be right back." Frank returned in record time, running up and down the stairs. I'm sure he never moves that fast when Julia calls him or sends him on an errand.

"I'll be crushed if you don't let me design it," he said opening a tablet he returned with.

"I've been working on these at the reception desk when I'm not busy," he said. He opened the sketch book to show me drawings of wedding dress designs that he had been making for me. "I've been working on these ever since I saw how romantic you two are together. I knew it was only a matter of time before Mr. Wonderful popped the question."

"How do you know it's not Dante?" I asked.

"Oh, ple-e-e-e-z-e," Frank said flipping open his

tablet.

"Okay, I guess everyone saw it but me," I said. "Frank, don't tell…"

"Her highness? She will be green with envy, and I'm not going to tell her, but I want to be there when you do. Deal?" Frank said rubbing his hands together in glee.

"Deal," I said looking through the designs. "Frank, these are exquisite. They're perfect. I don't want a long, ball gown, but something mid-calf like you have here."

"So, do you have a date already?" he asked after he went through showing me the designs and telling me why each one would look perfect on me. Each one was more beautiful than the previous one. All the drafts were exactly like the type of dress I had in mind.

"I don't know, really. Jiff is contacting this place his family owns to see when it's available. This won't be a year long, drawn out engagement. It could happen soon, maybe a month or two. I'll know more this evening when I meet him for dinner."

"A month or two!" Frank screamed holding his chest. "This doesn't give me much time since I'll have to do it on the down-low when the queen isn't here."

"I know, but do you think you can do it?" I asked in the most pitiful, pleading voice I could manage. "This isn't going to be a big, St. Louis Cathedral, thousand-person reception at a big downtown hotel ballroom. We are having a small wedding and reception, all of it, in the same place. I don't think we'll have more than seventy-five to eighty people there, and less if I get my way. We want it very intimate with close family and friends…and of course, my wedding dress designer."

"Of course. I can, and I will do it for you, my Princess," he said.

Frank never called me a Princess before but that is what I was feeling like.

"I'll finish these designs and maybe have one or two more for you to pick out as early as next week. Once you decide on the one you want, I can get it done in two weeks," Frank said. "I'll call you and let you know when she won't be here so we can look these over and you can decide. Do you have something in mind that you don't see here?"

"You've drawn versions of the exact dress that was in my head, and a few more," I said giving him a big hug.

Frank was a dynamo when it came to sewing and designing. He made almost all of Julia's clothes and they were stunning.

"Let me take your measurements right now so I'll have them and can get started once you select the one you want," he said pulling a tape from his organizer attached to his tablet.

I left Frank madly sketching away and walked out of Julia's Bed and Breakfast as if floating on air.

Chapter Twelve

Friday a.m.

THE NEXT DAY my cell phone rang bright and early. It was a call with Anthony's ID. When I answered, he launched into, "I saw your homeless guy's motorcycle parked on the side of a vacant building on France Road in the East. Take the France Road exit off I-10 southbound and you'll see his bike parked between two buildings about three blocks down. Everything around there is vacant and boarded up so look for his motorcycle. It's unmistakable—older bike but it's still RAD. Look for a Hell's Angel's sticker on the gas tank and you'll know you have the right place. He rides a 2011 Harley cruiser, soft tail, fat boy. It's a midnight blue, so dark it looks black and it's got some miles on it. It's visible from the street, but go slow. The building you're looking for is on the left. It's hard to make out any addresses because the numbers are missing or faded."

"You into bikes, Anthony?" I asked.

"I have always liked them," he said and hung up.

I called Jiff and he sounded like I just woke him up when he answered. We had a long night at his parents and he was supposed to go into work early. When I looked at my watch, I saw it was 7:00 am I said, "Can you go with me to New Orleans East? Anthony says the homeless guy from Ian's building is now living in an abandoned warehouse on France Road."

"Do not go by yourself," he said sounding much more awake. "I'll be there as soon as I can."

After I hung up with Jiff, I started looking up any photos Angie might have posted on Facebook of Ian, Phillip, Freddie, her dad and her uncle. I didn't have to look very far or very long. I printed out the ones I wanted to bring with me.

On the way, as Jiff drove, he updated me on the dates we could have for the wedding.

"Well, tomorrow, Saturday is open, but that might be kind of quick. I don't think we can get a license that fast, even with knowing a few judges," he said smiling and reaching over to take my hand.

"Yes, that is a tad too soon," I said. "What other dates were open?"

"There's one about five weeks out putting it the first week of September, but that's only available in the early afternoons. There's another open the first weekend in October. In October we can have Friday or Saturday night, if you want a night wedding," he said.

"I was thinking maybe October?"

"October is a good month in New Orleans," I said. "Not too hot and not really winter yet. I like October. It gives us more time to get things done. I hope I can find a caterer on such a short notice for a wedding."

"Let's go to my parents tonight for dinner and tell them what we are planning. My mother knows everybody in New Orleans, and I'm sure she will find you what you want. The event space has a list of caterers we regularly use, and I'm sure one of them will be available," he said. "I'm so excited we have a date now."

October was only nine weeks away and that nine weeks was going to fly, until I told my mother. Maybe I could get Frank to make her a dress. Wait, what? No, no, no! If Frank has to deal with my mother, he will never speak to me again and he might not finish my dress! She was going to have a fit if she didn't know early enough to get a dress that was appropriate for the "Mother of the Bride". I'll wait until the last minute and she'll think it's a party and not a wedding anyway. I sat pondering all the ways I had to deal with my mother, tell Dante and figure out how I was going to pay for all the things I needed to make this wedding not an embarrassment to Jiff's parents, who so graciously are giving us the venue for our big day.

"We drove to an abandoned warehouse on France

Road out toward Gentilly and the high rise bridge going over the Industrial Canal. Many buildings had been boarded up. Jiff drove slowly while I looked to see which building we were going to break into if no one came to peel off the plywood over the doorway when we knocked.

"That's it," I said pointing at a motorcycle parked behind a dumpster. It was hard to spot, but I was sure this was the right building.

Jiff and I walked up to where it looked like there was a loose piece of plywood to gain access. Before sticking our heads in, we yelled, "Hello, we'd like to talk to you. We're not here to kick you out."

We heard the sound of someone prying the plywood off the entry on the other side. When it moved there was a big, strong-looking guy standing there checking us out. He had to be 6'3" and was a burly sort of guy with a stocky build. He desperately needed a shave and his face was pock marked. I could see a long gray-haired ponytail from under the black-and-white bandana he wore covering the top of his head. It had a skull motif. He was wearing what I'd refer to as biker clothes: black T-shirt, leather vest, dirty blue jeans, and a chain from his belt loop to a pocket I assumed had his wallet attached to the other end. He had on thick boots and I could see several tats up and down both arms.

"I'm Brandy Alexander," I said extending my hand

to shake his. My hand hung out there a few seconds while he put the piece of plywood down he had been holding. He slowly reached to take my hand and gently shook it. "We wanted to ask if you are the person who saw the dynamite in the building on Richards Street while you were, uh, … living there."

He just stared at us at first. Finally, he said, "Nice to meet you, Ms. Alexander. You know, with that name you could make good money on Bourbon Street as a…"

"Okay, that's enough," Jiff said interrupting.

"I didn't mean no disrespect, Miss. I'm sorry," he said. He took a quick look in Jiff's direction adding, "Sorry, man."

I help up my hand to stop Jiff from saying anything else, and asked again, "I know you didn't. What's your name?"

"My God given name is Wallace, but my pals called me Chef," he said.

"Can we come in and talk to you?" I asked.

"Or we can talk right here," Jiff said.

Wallace stepped aside so I could enter. Jiff followed behind me.

There was a crate to sit on, a dirty mattress on the floor and a small table with the dirtiest, electric appliance covered in burned-on-food plugged into an extension cord that reached to an EXIT sign that was lit up. I only noticed it because the smell of burned food was coming from that direction.

"I only have one chair, but you can have it, Miss," he said nodding to the crate.

"I'm good standing," I said. "Thank you. So, Wallace…" I drifted off in mid-sentence because I heard a scratching sound and thought it was a rat. The sound was coming from a box near the mattress so I followed the sound over to it. When I peeked inside there was a baby squirrel rearranging some shredded newspaper. "Is this yours?" I asked.

"Kinda. I'm taking care of him until he can get out on his own. I found him at the last building I was living in. I couldn't leave him there with no one to feed him or he would'a died."

"He's cute," I said. "What are you feeding him?"

"Can we stay on the matter at hand?" Jiff asked in his most charming voice. "We'd like to ask you about the people you saw come pick up the dynamite at the other building. We think they are responsible for killing our friends in an explosion."

"Sure. Three guys came to pick up the boxes," Wallace said in answer to Jiff's questions as he took the squirrel out of the box and put him inside his T-shirt. I watched as the little bump moved around and then settled where Wallace's shirt tucked into his jeans. He turned to me and said, "I feed him peanuts I buy for him."

"Was it any of these people?" I asked showing him Freddie's picture posted on Instagram.

Wallace said, "Yeah man. That's Coke Bottle Freddie. I knew him when we rode together."

"Did you talk to him, ask him about the dynamite, like what was he gonna do with it?" Jiff asked.

"He didn't see me. I was upstairs hiding in a bathroom. Freddie had two guys with him. One was an older guy. I've never seen him before."

I showed some Facebook photos of Angie's dad, her uncle and Phillip. Wallace pointed to a photo of Angie's uncle and said it looked like the older man. Wallace said he never saw anyone who looked like Phillip.

"There was another guy with them. I didn't get a good look at him. He was doing most of the work, carrying the boxes outside to a car," he said. "He looked like a biker that might be an old friend of Coke Bottle Freddie. I didn't get a good look at him so I can't be sure, but he had club tats on his arms. He was wearing a sleeveless shirt and leathers."

"Was anyone else with them? Driving the car or just giving orders?" I asked.

"The old guy gave the orders. When they loaded up the car, I saw a woman, small, angry-looking woman, with them waiting outside. I'm not sure but I think she was Coke Bottle Freddie's sister. I haven't seen her in a long time. She looked a lot more respectable that day than when I last saw her. I didn't get a really good look at her, but she rode on the back of my bike from time to time." He hurried to add, "But she wasn't my old lady or nuttin'. She moved around from biker to biker, if you know what I mean."

"Yeah, I think I know what you mean, Wallace," I said while I watched Jiff move around the back of Wallace to keep a better eye on him.

"Call me Chef," he said. "I like it better than Wallace."

"So how did you get the name Chef?" I asked. Curious minds needed to know. As awful as he looked, I didn't feel threatened by Wallace, or Chef. I sensed Jiff was feeling and acting threatened enough for both of us.

"Cuz I like to cook and I always cooked for the gang when we stopped somewhere. I also cooked meth for our brothers in the gang, so I was called Chef for that reason too," he said. "Now I peel peanuts for this little guy." The squirrel has climbed up his shirt and stuck his head out under Chef's chin. He was now holding the squirrel in one giant, greasy looking hand and stroking him with his index finger on the other hand.

"So, do you miss that? Cooking...food...meth,

riding with your biker pals?" I asked and over Wallace's shoulder I could see Jiff doing a giant eye roll that caused his head to roll with it.

"No Ma'am. I've done a lot of bad stuff in my life," Wallace said. "It got me in a lot of trouble. Not only did I hurt a lot of people, but I caused their families pain. I wish I could make it up some kinda way. I'm sorry I cooked meth, but I did like cooking food. I wish I could make amends for the meth I cooked and the bad things I done."

"What about the gang lifestyle? Don't you miss riding on your, your…"

"Harley."

"Yes, your Harley motorcycle. Don't you miss riding that?"

"No, I still have my bike. I miss having a hot mama hanging onto me, but I'm not missing riding with the gang. Even as a member, you had to be careful who you might tick off. Sometimes a brother's ol' lady hopped on the back of my bike when she was ticked at her old' man. We didn't have marriages, or nuttin like that. You just rode with who you wanted to ride with, and that was cool for a while. It made for some interesting fights over dinner and at bars—waiting to see who left with who."

"I bet it did," I said.

"Now, this is my riding partner," he said nodding

at the baby squirrel. "I put him inside my shirt and he sits there until we get where I'm going. I'm afraid to leave him here alone."

Even though I could see Jiff tapping his watch over Wallace's shoulder, I wanted more information I thought this guy could have. He was scary to look at, but he was nice to talk to, and the gentle way he handled the baby squirrel impressed me. "What did you do when you were with the Hell's Angels to get yourself incarcerated?" I asked.

Jiff looked at me as if to ask, REALLY, with his eyes while holding up one arm and tapping his watch with the other hand, like I couldn't see him doing it without waving his arms around.

I ignored him.

"Well, I was doing a lot of meth in those days. So was Freddie. We decided to steal a boat motor from this repair shop out on Paris Road. We were so high, we thought it was midnight. Turns out it was five o'clock on a Friday. There was a million people around coming to get their repaired engines for weekend boating. The owner saw us and called the police. Freddie jumped in the canal in the back of the place and swam away from the cops. The cops didn't want to go in after him and I think they thought he would drown since we both was so messed up. I got nailed and was arrested. I had a couple of other infractions so I did time."

"Are you still doing...infractions?" I asked.

"No, I got clean in prison," he said. "I worked in the kitchen, out of general population."

"Wallace, sorry, Chef, are you going to be here a few more days?" I asked.

"I'll be here until someone or the police run me out," he said.

"Would you be willing to testify who you saw taking the dynamite out of that other building?" I asked. "This could start you on the road to making amends. It's sort of paying it forward. You could help stop other people getting hurt by those who are still doing the bad stuff like you once did."

Wallace thought a minute. His face got serious, so serious he looked more frightening. I started to worry he might squeeze the baby squirrel. Then he said, "Yes. Yes, I'll talk to whoever you want me to and tell them who and what I saw."

"Okay, I'll be back, but here's my cell number. If you move, call me and let me know how to find you," I said. I slipped him a twenty-dollar bill with the paper I wrote my cell number on.

"I don't have no cell phone. I'm looking for a job and once I have a job I can find someplace to live. My sister let me sleep on her sofa for a week when I got outta prison, but she said I scared her two little girls so

I can't stay there no more. I'll find a way to call you if I get tossed outta here," he said.

"I might know someone who will give you a job on a trial basis," I said. "So keep in touch with me."

"I'd be grateful for any help you throw my way, Miss. Thank you," he said.

Once we left the building, I don't think we were out of earshot when Jiff exploded with, "What are you thinking? He could've pulled a knife on us and stabbed us, or shot us, or just killed us with his bare hands. Did you see the size of them?"

"Did that guy look like he was going to stab anyone? I don't think he even had a knife. Usually you are much more open-minded about all kinds of people," I said. "Besides, he has a squirrel."

"You wanna get a gang banger—meth-head a job?" he squawked.

"A retired biker—squirrel loving—no longer a meth cook, a job. You need to think more positive if we're going to find Ian and Sophie's killers."

"A job with who? They will never speak to you again if you talk someone into hiring him," he said all in one breath.

"With the police. A job with the police...as an informer. He cooks so maybe he can work as a cook for the police or a fire station and help them find these meth houses. If Wallace really wants to make amends, that's how he can do it," I said. "I have a good feeling about the guy."

He said, "Work for a police department? On this planet?"

"I have one in mind."

"If it's with who I'm thinking, Dante will never go for it," he said.

"That's not who I'm going to ask."

Jiff was right. Dante was never going to go for this, so I called Detective Taylor. Jiff drove us back to my car and sat next to me, just shaking his head as if defeat was eminent. When Taylor picked up my call, he answered like he always does, "Miss Alexander, what can I do for you, today?"

"I called to do something for you," I said.

"Do something for me? Has the world spun off its axis?" he said. "Let me look out of the window and see if it's coming to an end."

"Well, I called to give you information and to get your opinion on something," I said. "How does the NOPD deal with informants? Can you actually get them jobs somewhere?"

"De-p-e-e-e-n-ds…" Taylor answered slowly, dragging out the word. I could imagine he was squinting his eyes and wondering what I wanted with a slight turn of his head at the other end of the phone.

"It depends on the information?"

"Y-e-e-e-e-s...," he said.

"Stop talking like that," I said. "The guy who can ID the suspect in the Ian Saucier murder is currently homeless and living in a vacant building." No use unloading all the info on Wallace at one time. It might be too much for Taylor and then he wouldn't want to help or ask Dante. "This homeless guy, Wallace, saw who came and got the dynamite the day before the barge explosion on the 4th of July."

"Let's see how reliable this guy, this homeless guy, is and then we can talk informer and job," Taylor said.

"Well, can you at least ask Dante if he would consider using this guy as an informant?"

"Informant on what? On who? I need some particulars before I go to the boss," he said.

Then I heard Dante's voice say Taylor's name. I could hear Taylor put the phone against his hand or chest followed by Dante's muffled voice.

"Here's the Captain now. You can ask him yourself," he said and the next voice I heard was Dante's.

Uh oh. I wasn't prepared to talk to him.

"Hey Dante. I might have a good source of information for you. He claims he saw the guys who picked up dynamite the day before the 4th," I said talking to fast. "He's homeless and needs a job, and he has other information that could lead to future arrests."

"Other information? Like what?" Dante asked.

"He used to be the cook in a motorcycle group he rode with. He likes to cook," I said trying to ease into this. I would have had much better luck if I had gone straight to see Dante and asked him in person.

"Motorcycle group? Like a gang? The only cooks in gangs are meth cooks. I've never seen a biker gang pulling a food truck behind them. Did this guy cook meth? You want me to pay an informer for cooking meth?" Dante ranted.

Then, Taylor was back on the phone, "Miss Alexander, we need to talk to that homeless guy, so…"

"Remind me never to ask for your help again, especially with…with… my plans," I said cutting him off, and hung up.

"So-o-o-o how did that go for ya?" Jiff asked.

"It went much better when I had the conversation with him in my head," I said. "You know, Julia met Frank in central lockup and hired him. Maybe she'll hire Wallace."

"I'll let you handle that request by yourself," he said. "I'll drop you off at Julia's. Use the office account to get a taxi back to your car. I've got to get back to finish some interrogatories for a case."

After giving Jiff a quick kiss goodbye, I walked up the brick sidewalk and steps to Julia's guest house for the second time in as many days.

"Well, well, look who's here," Frank said in a loud

voice I could only imagine was for Julia's benefit. He had on the same outfit as yesterday but today he added a beret.

"I took your suggestion and added this," he whispered to me pointing to the beret on his head.

I gave him a thumbs up. "Frank, I'm here to see Julia. Is she in?" I asked. I didn't have to raise my voice as Julia had supersonic hearing.

He nodded indicating she was upstairs.

I said. "Take me to her highness."

I followed Frank upstairs.

The door to her office/boudoir was open, and she was standing in between the two rooms trying on hats—the hats I had seen yesterday.

"Brandy," Julia said. "You're just in time. You can help me decide on what hat to wear to a luncheon I was invited to. It's at the Ritz. I'm now on a list of New Orleans businesswomen who get invited to a monthly luncheon."

It was always all about Julia. She didn't ask why I stopped by and I'm not sure she ever would. I'd have to find a way to broach the subject of Wallace as a cook for the guest house.

"Pick the one that doesn't give you a headache if you have to keep it on for more than an hour," I said.

"That's what I told her," Frank said.

Julia turned to look at me. She had a puzzled expression on her face and I assumed it was from her trying to figure out how long the luncheon was going to last. Instead, she said, "You look different."

"I told her that too. Brandy looks happy, not that you would recognize happy," he said to Julia.

"Frank," Julia snapped as she whipped her hat-wearing head in his direction.

Frank scurried out of the room saying, "And, I'm going back down to the reception desk."

"I guess I'm in a good mood," I said. It was w-a-a-a-a-y too early to tell Julia about my engagement with Jiff. October was a good two months away and she had plenty of time to out me with my mother. I knew Frank could keep a secret if you threatened him under the penalty of death or that I'd tell Julia he used her makeup. Julia had ways to make Frank talk, like she could threaten him with discontinuing his employment if she thought he knew something she didn't. It was time to redirect her attention. "Look, I came here to ask you if you need a cook."

"A cook? Frank manages for the little we do here for breakfast, coffee and happy hour. Why?" Julia asked still scrutinizing my face.

"I met a guy who is down on his luck. Well, he's down on his luck because he's out of prison and needs a job. He used to be a cook," I said leaving out the meth part. "You met Frank while you were...well, you gave

Frank a job and look how well that worked out."

"That's hardly the sales pitch to recommend some-one," she said. "Using Frank as an example is only going to hurt his chances. Anyway, this is the slow time of the year and I can't take on another employee right now. In the fall, maybe, if he's still needs a job."

"Okay, I'll keep that in mind," I said. Well, she didn't say no to the idea, just that the timing was bad.

"Are you going on a trip? Or did you just get back from a trip? You look like you're relaxed. Did Jiff take you somewhere?" she asked.

"No, we haven't been on a trip, but we're making plans. Nothing is confirmed yet," I said. "I'll tell you as soon as I know. Gotta run."

Downstairs, I started to call the taxi service from reception when Frank walked up

"She started asking questions," I whispered to Frank.

"She's going to that luncheon on Monday. Call me after you look at these and tell me what you like or want changed. I did a few more yesterday after you left. Come on Monday at lunchtime, and we'll get started. She'll never know," he said.

"Okay," I said leaving as I got the text from the car service.

Friday p.m.

AFTER LEAVING JULIA'S guest house I went to my office thinking I'd get a jumpstart on next week. After I closed all my files I started searching on the Internet for houses for sale. There were so many questions regarding price range, square footage and area of the city I almost gave up. Then an elegant Victorian for sale uptown caught my eye. I printed it all out to show Jiff this evening on our way to his parents' home for dinner. It was almost 3:30 p.m.. After all, this was a Friday afternoon in New Orleans. Very few returned to the office after a late lunch on the last day of the work week. It was summer and many had left for their beach or weekend homes along the Gulf Coast. It did feel like we invented the four-and-a-half day-work week.

I went home, relaxed a bit, and decided what to wear to the Jiff's parents' house for dinner to make our announcement. My nerves were starting to remind me of the big step we were taking. While I was excited to tell his parents, that only meant the clock was ticking louder reminding me it would be time...soon...to tell my parents. To relax, I took Meaux and Isabella for an afternoon stroll. It was 5:30 p.m. when my cell phone rang.

"Hey," I answered.

"I'm ready to leave my office. Do you want me to come by to pick you up to go to my parent's for dinner?" he said. "I'm starving."

"I came home early," I said. "Can you pick me up here? I needed to go home first to feed Meaux and Isabella and I wanted to freshen up."

"Let's bring Isabella and Meaux," he said. "I'll see you in a few."

When I saw him pull up, we were ready to go.

When I reached the car, Jiff gave me a hug saying, "I just can't imagine how Sophie or Ian would feel knowing what happened to the other one. I can't stop thinking about them."

"Well, I can't stop thinking about them either. "I hope your parents are expecting us, all of us." I nodded toward the two at the end of their leashes.

"They are. My parents love dogs," Jiff smiled and helped me get Meaux and Isabella into the back seat. "They will be so thrilled. They love you."

"I started looking for a place for us," I said. "I found something that has an open house this Sunday if you think you're interested. I want to drive past this house before we go to your parents. It's on the way." I said handing him a printout of the Victorian I liked.

"Where is it?" he asked, looking at the photos and printout.

The home was on Prytania Street, in a lovely section of the Garden District. Jiff noticed there was a driveway and three car garage across the back of the property. I noticed the wide, front porch and swing.

On top of the FOR SALE sign there was a rider indicating an Open House. "See, there's an open house this Sunday. Let's come to it, and look around," I said.

"Perfect," Jiff said squeezing my hand.

We sat in the car looking at the house and telling each other things about it we liked. It was beautiful with a large side yard complete with a gazebo that appeared well maintained from the outside. I was in love with it already.

"Let's go eat before someone inside calls the police because we are loitering here," I said.

"No one calls the police on what might be a potential buy in front of a house with a FOR SALE sign," Jiff said laughing. "Let's go get Meaux introduced to the family. They love Isabella and will love him too. It's a good time to let Meaux meet his future in-laws. I hope he likes them!"

Chapter Thirteen

Friday p.m.

JIFF'S FATHER GREETED us at the front door. He shook his son's hand, gave me a big hug, and then bent down to pet Isabella and ask, "Who do we have here?" he asked as he reached for Meaux.

"Well, we thought you should meet Brandy's family," Jiff said. "This is Meaux."

"Excellent idea!" his dad said. "What a handsome Schnauzer he is. Looks like he's the perfect companion for Isabella."

"Yes, it was love at first sight for Isabella. Kinda like me," Jiff said putting his arm around me.

Jiff obviously missed the deer in the headlights look on my face at the mere mention of our human families meeting. OMG! What if his parents wanted to meet my parents before the October date? That just could not happen.

Jiff's mother came into the parlor and gave me a hug. I had met his mother, father, and brothers right after we started dating at their home uptown. They lived on Audubon Place, a private street with its own gated entrance manned by 24-hour security. All the mansions on this prestigious block were well over two hundred years old and had been passed down in families through generations. Jiff's parents lived in the largest estate on the corner of Audubon Place and St. Charles Avenue.

"I hope you're staying for dinner," Jiff's mother said just as a man dressed as a butler entered with a tray of champagne flutes filled with what I was sure was very expensive bubbly.

"Yes, Mother, we are," Jiff said. "I told you we had something we wanted to tell you. I'm sure you've guessed based on the champagne Mr. Marshall is passing around.

"Life is too short not to celebrate all things, like my son coming to dinner," she said smiling and raising her glass. "And meeting Meaux."

The room was very quiet when Mr. Marshall left, and with Jiff's parents looking back and forth to each of us. His dad finally said, "We're waiting…"

"I've asked Brandy and Meaux to marry me," he said. His mother grabbed her chest with her free hand and both his parents smiled broadly. Jiff added, "They both said yes."

Hugs were exchanged all around and Meaux and

Isabella barked, adding to the excitement.

"Sit down, sit down, and tell us your plans," Jiff's dad said. "I'm sure I speak for your mother as well as myself when I say we couldn't be happier for you, son. Our family is happy to welcome you, Brandy, into our fold."

Jiff said he had checked into the Aucoin House in the French Quarter and there was a date in October he wanted to schedule for our wedding.

"This October?" Mrs. Heinkel asked.

"Yes, Brandy and I are looking for a house together and with our jobs we don't have a lot of time to spend on making endless arrangements. Most of it will fall on Brandy and we talked about what was important to us and we decided we want to merge the engagement announcement along with the wedding," Jiff said as his parents listened.

"We eloped," his mother said. "I get it. Families with good intentions can create saga and drama in your marriage before it starts. My mother was a difficult and overbearing woman. I didn't want her planning my wedding. So, his mother suggested we elope and it was the perfect solution. Do what your heart tells you."

Was this woman physic or what?

"We both have tons of friends and a lot of family so we didn't want to get into a huge reception. I'd like it to be special and shared with those who mean the most to us," I said.

"Well, you've got yourself a smart one here," Mr. Heinkel said. "Of course, you can have the Aucoin House and all of the services we use are available to you as well. If you want a particular date, let me know and we'll arrange it."

"Dad, I've checked and the October date is open. That's why we picked it," Jiff said. "Mom, I told Brandy you can suggest a caterer or two she might want to interview."

"I would be thrilled to make a recommendation for you and your mother to talk to," Mrs. Heinkel said.

"I…will be making all the arrangements myself," I said. "I no longer live at home so I will not be expecting my parents to feel obligated financially. I only expect them to attend our wedding."

Mrs. Heinkel was a gem. She picked up on any issues and graciously sailed past them.

"Well, I'm happy to help, recommend, or go with you. Let me know when you are ready to select food, cake, flowers, whatever you need," she said.

"Even having our wedding as a small affair will be challenging, so I'll gladly accept your offer to help me make good choices," I said. "I'm particularly worried about ordering food for the reception following the exchange of our vows."

"My mother is the queen of parties and ordering

the right food," Jiff said.

"I think as a working woman you will find Aucoin House can offer you everything you want or need for your wedding. If you absolutely want to use another vendor, you will not hurt our feelings. Everything for parties, weddings, rehearsals, anything is available to you and all the vendors we use are noted for their dependability and stellar product they deliver."

"That sounds incredibly time saving," I said. "Thank you. Thank you both."

"We should make an appointment to go there and see Christine so she can tell you what we offer. We've never not been able to accommodate brides, so I know we will not disappoint you with whatever you have in mind. In fact, we just won't let that happen," she said smiling and hugging me again.

"I will gladly accept your help meeting with Christine and talking about everything I need to do to make this happen in a beautiful, understated way," I said.

"I'll call her tomorrow and see what dates and times she is available next week and then you let me know which date works best for you, okay?"

"That is perfect. I really wasn't sure where to start, or what to order first. I'm already feeling less stressed over this," I said.

We moved to the dining room when Mr. Marshall came back to take drink orders and announced dinner was ready to be served. My stress level continued to ratchet itself down as the evening progressed, mainly because no one suggested we have a meet and greet with both sets of parents. I'm sure Mrs. Heinkel figured that wasn't a great idea when I said my mother would not be helping me in anyway.

As we left for the night, Mrs. Heinkel walked me to the door with her arm around my shoulders and said, "Anything you need, just ask. I won't interfere or offer suggestions unless you ask me. Please know, I'd be ecstatic to help with anything. I have five boys and one girl. I will have very little, if any, involvement other than to attend the weddings of my sons, and our daughter has a career that doesn't encourage dating so it doesn't look like there's a marriage in her foreseeable future, so I would be happy to help you with anything."

Wow, I felt like I was marrying into the Royal Family.

Chapter Fourteen

Saturday a.m.

IT WASN'T UNTIL Saturday morning that I came down from the cloud nine ride with the Heinkels. Jiff was up early checking his emails for scans from Ed Chauvin.

At breakfast I said, "Back to the matter at hand."

Jiff looked up with a 'huh?' expression over his coffee.

"Our pseudo day job of crime solving…that matter at hand," I said. "I feel like we're missing something. Like two bodies that should have been found in an explosion or house fire—Ian and Sophie. Where are they? Why haven't any of their remains been found?"

"I don't know," he said. "I don't like thinking about it. They were friends."

"Yes, it would be hard to think about friends lost under circumstances like that," I said.

"I woke up thinking about that house on Prytania. Still want to go see it?" Jiff asked.

"Absolutely," I said and gave him a big hug and a kiss. "I'm making eggs for breakfast, want some?"

"Yeah, thanks," he said.

As I served him the eggs I said, "I have a feeling, nothing I can prove, but a feeling that Ian and Sophie are still alive."

"What? How can you say that?" Jiff asked as he looked up from staring in his coffee.

"Because, you said so yourself... Ian was smart. Maybe he figured out what was going on. He must have thought they were in danger. He wrote you that note knowing he was going to see you in a couple of days and he took out those life insurance policies."

"Now you're guessing," Jiff said. "There isn't enough forensic evidence to draw a conclusion yet."

"Yes, but it's an educated guess based on that fact. There isn't any forensic evidence of bodies matching Sophie or Ian. To me, no evidence is evidence of something else. The body in the house fire is male so we know it's not Sophie. We know Ian was taken out to the fireworks barge because we have an eyewitness, Jack, who saw him leave and saw Freddie come back without him. Ian, nor any part of Ian, has ever been found. We don't have anything other than the two explosions happening almost at the exact same time. You know neither of us believes in coincidence," I said.

"So, are you saying whoever planned these so-called

accidents somehow bungled them by causing them to happen at the same time?" he asked.

"Yes. That's what I'm saying," I said.

"Then why hasn't Ian or Sophie come forward or tried to contact me, at least?" he asked.

"Maybe he's waiting for the truth to come out. If they come forward, he'll be looked at for the barge explosion and who knows what they will try to pin on him with his house burning down at the same time," I said. "We know that was arson and if someone is killed in the commission of a felony, then homicide is added to the list. Those insurance policies guarantee an investigation. They will send their own investigators and lean on the police not to jump to an accidental death conclusion."

"I didn't think of that, but you're right. Especially with both happening at the same time. The police will think Ian killed Sophie for the money and staged his own death. If she were around, the police would think she had something to do with Ian's death. Either or both of them would be suspect number one," Jiff said, holding his chin in one hand with his elbow in the other.

Right now, everyone is focused on Phillip and Angie over the life insurance, and not the issues surrounding the lab. So let's focus on the lab," I said, "and Angie."

"I need to go into my office and print out the files Ed Chauvin is sending. It will take a while to go through them and draft a complaint on Phillip's behalf to exonerate him," Jiff said.

"And?"

"And, he's emailing me the photos he has taken over the years and recent lab results from those very labs Phillip said they had to use. He said he'd get them all scanned in to send to me over the weekend from his home. He won't do anything at the office. He thinks it's bugged," Jiff said. "He said he was calling me on a burner phone. I need to check my emails."

"Give the man some time," I said. "His workweek just ended, and I'm sure he'd like to have supper too. He might not start sending it until later today or tomorrow."

"Yes, you're right," he said giving me a hug.

"What did you think of that house we drove by?"

"I can't wait to see it," he said looking around my place. "You already have some nice antique pieces that would look great in there."

"Do you think it's too big?" I asked.

"No. My parents have a huge house plus an attic full of antique furniture. They're saving it for one of us to take and use when we need it," he said. "But if you don't like any of it we don't have to take it."

"I think antiques or vintage furniture would look

great in a Victorian or any uptown home we buy," I said smiling. "I can't wait to go shopping in their attic!"

"No matter how big the house we buy, we'll have it filled up in no time. That's how it works," Jiff said smiling at me. Then he started to call someone on his cell.

"Who are you calling?"

"The office. I'm getting someone to check my emails and call me if something comes in from Ed Chauvin. Then I'll go into the office and start working on it. Until then, let's go see that house. I want to see it today, before the Open House tomorrow, don't you?" he asked.

I listened while he made an appointment to view the home in two hours, confirming the time out loud while I nodded in agreement. Oh boy, we were going to look at a house to buy together. My knees felt a little shaky so I sat down. Jiff went straight back to the computer to check the email again.

THE AGENT MET us at the Prytania House and showed us through it. Everything about it was exactly as I imagined it would look and then some. We both fell in love at first sight. The ceilings all had beautiful medallions around the chandeliers, the rooms were tall, oversized and well-appointed with marble fireplaces. Except for a few bold colors painted in bedrooms—

there were five—there was nothing about the house I didn't like. Jiff pointed out, "It's only paint. We'll get someone to paint it the color you want."

The entry had a grand staircase to the second floor with a second stairwell at the back of the house that was more functional and out of view from the main part of the house.

There was a grand wrap-around porch and the house sat on a double lot that had a wrought iron fence surrounding the property. There was space enough for Meaux, Isabella and all their Schnauzer friends with tons of flowers, azaleas and trees for a yard party.

We followed the agent back to her office and Jiff said we wanted to put in an offer.

When I walked out of the real estate office, I got weak in the knees. "What if they accept our offer?" I asked him hearing a tremble in my own voice.

"Well, that is sort of what we want to happen. We hope they do, or come back with a counter that we're willing and able to pay." Taking my hand, he said, "This is so exciting. Let's have lunch."

Terrifying was more like it. I didn't think I could eat since there was a knot in my stomach where food should want to go. Is there anything that can make a man not want to eat? We walked to a restaurant on Magazine, a block or so over on the corner. It was a cute little French restaurant we've been to in the past. It felt good to sit and reflect on this all-important moment in our life, but I could not think of eating food.

Jiff shared with me what he thought would look great in the house that was in his parents' attic. I told him where I thought some of my antiques might work. I ordered a salad and picked at it while Jiff got an enormous hamburger with a mountain of fries. As we were leaving, he got a call from his office.

Michelle said emails were coming in from an Ed Chauvin and she thought he might want to see them.

Jiff told her, "Start printing them out. I'm on my way." To me he said after he hung up, "There's a ton of files with photos, documents and reports. This will take a while to go through." He looked at his watch. "I'll probably work late and go back in early tomorrow to get this ready for Monday. I'm sorry, but you're on your own, unless the realtor calls. Then call me and let me know if they accept our offer."

With that he took off for his office, leaving me to wonder if home ownership was in my immediate future.

Several hours later, Jiff called to update me on the Chauvin files. "There are over fifty years of photos, lab results, and statements from Ed Chauvin documenting all that he collected showing when and where. He has duplicate samples of the ones sent to that lab, and he says he will sign an affidavit to all of it. He's asking me not give it to the EPA counsel until next week. That gives me a day to get a draft of what I want to send to the EPA with the complaint."

"I can bring you dinner if you're pulling a late night," I said.

"I'll let you know. We can always get something delivered," he said. "Hear anything on the house?"

"Nothing yet from the realtor on the offer," I said.

"Wait a sec," Jiff said. "There's also an email here from Michelle sent late last night. She has proof that Angie's dad, her uncle, and Freddie are getting payments from the lab in question being direct deposited into their checking accounts. The EPA office should be paying the lab for the work, which they are. So this looks like kickbacks. This should prove they had motive to kill Ian, Sophie, and try to kill Phillip. We need to give this to the police and the District Attorney's office. It certainly presents another theory on why Ian was murdered."

"With Wallace testifying he saw them moving dynamite and this information from Ed Chauvin, will this exonerate Phillip from suspicion?" I asked.

"First, we need to get "Squirrel Man" to the police station to talk to them. He's not the most reliable looking witness and his domicile keeps moving so he could vanish again. Second, you need to get them to listen to him. The second one might be harder than the first," Jiff said.

I spent an anxious day waiting to hear from the realtor. We had given them overnight to accept or reject our offer. The terrifying jolts of reality on buying this home and being responsible for the financial obligation interrupted moments of sheer bliss thinking how our new family would live in it together. I started binging on home improvement shows with Meaux and Isabella. I fell asleep on the sofa, and Suzanne woke me up when she came in from work around 4:00 am She shuffled me off to my bedroom with the dogs. After two hours of fitfully trying to fall back asleep, I realized I was fully awake at 6:00 am on Sunday morning, the time the alarm normally wakes me during the work week. I was pinned under the sheets with a dog on either side of me so turning was not an option. Even getting out of bed was going to take some effort and disturbing a sleeping dog. The dogs were sleeping so soundly, I heard Meaux softly snoring, and I didn't want to wake them.

In addition to worrying over the offer on the house, I had little snippets of dreams where Wallace moved again and I was not able to find him. In one snippet, there was Phillip in jail with Angie laughing at him over the phone on visitor's day through the glass. I reached for my cell on the nightstand so I could Google places open on Sunday where I could buy a burner phone for him. This way I didn't have to disturb Meaux and Isabella. Sunday hours ranged from opening at 10:00 am to noon.

My cell phone rang, and caller ID said it was Detective Taylor.

I answered saying, "This is a tad early, Detective. What can I do for you?"

"No, Miss Alexander I called to tell you something...and, well...ask you something also. The DNA found in the house fire is Fred Finkelstein, Jr. His DNA was on file from when he was arrested for drugs over the last few years. I thought you would like to know," he said.

"Wow, that's Angie's brother and Phillip's brother-in-law. I knew he had tangled with the law, just didn't know to what extent. Thanks. Now, ask me what you really called about," I said.

"I'd like to talk to the homeless guy you said saw someone pick up the dynamite at the building he was sleeping in—you know, the building Ian Saucier and Phillip Wilson own."

"Lucky for you, I found him...again. I was going to drop off a phone to him this morning, but I don't have a burner in my inventory at home so I've got to wait until a store opens."

"I've got one I can give you," Taylor said. "I'll

swing by your house and drop it off to you. I'll go with you if you are worried about going alone."

"No. I'm afraid you will scare him off. I've seen how you stare at suspects," I said.

"I don't stare. I study," he said. "I'll just follow you and make sure you'll be safe."

"You stare. I'm probably safer with him than with you. I'm guessing that if I insist you not follow me, you will anyway," I said.

"You trust this guy? I ran his name. He's got a sheet as long as your arm. I really think I ought to go with you, and yes, I'm going to follow you anyway," he said, "from a safe distance."

"You can follow me…but you have to wait outside at a very safe distance so he doesn't see you," I said.

"I'd like to talk to him and see if he's anywhere near reliable before we ask him to come to the station. Do you want the Captain to take my head off for suggesting we use a meth head as a witness?" Detective Taylor asked.

"Well, I can't make any promises, but I'll ask if he'll talk to you when we get there."

As I drove up, I saw Wallace coming out of the building and getting on his motorcycle. I had Taylor on the cell phone telling him to park a block or so away so he didn't threaten Wallace. I said I'd call him over once I cleared it with Wallace. Taylor discreetly parked a block away, maintaining a line of vision direct to the building I told him I was going to.

"Hey, Wallace," I yelled before he kick-started his Harley and drowned me out.

"Oh, hey. What brings you here so early?" he asked turning to look at me.

"I was out running errands and since it looks like you're leaving, I wanted you to be able to stay in touch with me in case you had to relocate," I said giving him the burner cell. "This is for you and my number is programmed in there already."

"Gee, that's really nice of you," he said checking out the phone.

Okay, I wasn't running errands anywhere near this part of the city, but Wallace did not need to know that. "If you have to call the police, call 911 and ask for Detective Taylor. I've told him about you and he wants to speak with you," I said. When I saw the startled look on Wallace's face, I added, "I'll go with you to tell the police what you saw. You will not be in trouble. The guy that came with me the time we met is my boyfriend and he's an attorney, a criminal attorney. He could come with us and represent you, but only if you want him to." I paused to let it sink in. "Do you trust me?"

"Yes," he said nodding his head as if still processing what I told him.

"I have a minute, so tell me more about how you know Freddie and his sister, Angie. That's if you have time right now," I said.

Wallace explained more about his acquaintance with Coke Bottle Freddie, "Freddie's claim to fame was helping friends by setting gasoline or gas fires for insurance money. Of course, he burned himself very badly once from the gasoline vapors after he doused a car with it and forgot a match or lighter. So he went back to his car, found a match, then when he lit it, the fumes ignited and took all the hair on his face and some of his head off. Eyebrows, mustache, beard, hair on the front of his head, so it looked like he had a ponytail that started from hair growing out the back of his head." Wallace laughed adding, "He looked really weird for a long time and took a lot of teasing over it."

Wallace asked me what time was it and I told him the cell phone I gave him had a clock in it and it was almost 8:00.

"I need to get over to the mission on Camp Street. They find work for us. Those of us who get there early get assigned better jobs," he said.

"Okay, but I'm going to talk to a friend of mine at the police department and see when they can meet with us," I said.

"I think they might take me more seriously if you're with me," he said looking down at his feet. "The mission will pay me this afternoon for work I did this week, so I can buy a clean shirt and pants at a thrift store. I'll buy what I need after work today so don't make it before tomorrow. I'll go to the mission and shower, shave, and put on the clean clothes if you could pick me up there or I'll meet you. Either way, I'll look more presentable."

"Yes, call me this evening after you leave work and let me know you found what you need or want to wear for tomorrow," I said. "I can spot you a few bucks if you're short on what you need to get."

"Thank you for the offer but I should be fine. I'll give you a call later today," Wallace said kicking his bike alive with a thunderous blast. He put on his black helmet with worn, faded decals of a skull with cross-bones and rode off in a roar. Yes, I thought, it might be better if I went with him.

I saw my cell phone was ringing before I heard it.

"I thought you were gonna call me to talk to him?" Taylor sounded incredulous on the other end.

"He has a job to get to and he wanted to buy some clean clothes to wear before speaking to the police. He has an idea of what you might think about anything he has to say with the way he looks now. Don't you agree?" I said. "I'm supposed to pick him up tomorrow at his work and bring him to the station to talk to you."

"Or I can meet both of you at his workplace," Taylor offered.

Thinking many of the men, like Wallace, at the mission might be dodging the police, I said, "I'll ask but it might not help his long-term employment if the police come calling for him. Know what I mean?"

"You have a point."

"I'll call you and either bring him to you or you can meet us somewhere," I said.

As IT GOT closer to the dinner hour, which was any time after 7:00 p.m. for Jiff, my cell phone rang.

"I can't make dinner tonight. I'll be pulling an all-nighter and maybe one tomorrow night if I don't finish," he said.

I told Jiff about giving Wallace a phone, Taylor, and the plan to bring Wallace to the station.

"I spent most of the day going over those files Ed Chauvin sent and making a case against the lab with Michelle's research on Angie, Angie's father, her uncle, and her brother. I can make a case proving they were all taking payoffs," he said. "I'm calling the EPA in the morning. We still need more proof that one of them tried to kill Ian and Sophie. Right now, all we have is speculation."

"I think Wallace can put them there with the dy-namite. I'm hoping the insurance investigation turns up the heat on Angie," I said.

"Yes, but it's also turning it up on Phillip. I need to find concrete evidence to exonerate him," Jiff said.

"Think about it," I said. "Ian sees the writing on the wall with the labs so he gets life insurance policies for Sophie's protection in case something happens to him, but that's like waving a flag in front of Angie."

"What did Esme say…Angie pounced on Phillip when she met him like she pounced on making the claim on Ian," Jiff said.

"Angie gets her brother to plant dynamite in the 4th of July display which would blow up the barge at the same time as the house burns. Phillip was supposed to be there with Ian on the barge but had to run down to the riverfront. Phillip also said Ian took Freddie with him to help. I wonder if Angie knew that Phillip wasn't going to be with Ian. Wallace said Freddie's claim to fame was fires so it isn't a stretch he made the leap to explosions."

"Proving it will be tough," Jiff said.

"Maybe not if the police find the weakest link in the lab hustle. My money is on Freddie or Angie. She isn't going to go to jail for her brother, her dad or her uncle," I said.

"We still need to tie one of them to the house fire," Jiff said. "We haven't received the report from the Arson Investigator yet."

We sat there thinking and then I said, "When

Freddie took Ian to the barge, he left him there knowing there was dynamite. Given his interest in all things "fuego", maybe he wanted to see the house blow up so he called a pal to come pick him up and take him over to the house. When it didn't blow, maybe Freddie opened the door to see why. Remember the big explosion we heard right before the barge blew? I think there was an explosion at Ian's house, then the fire, not the fire first followed by an explosion. According to Wallace it would not be the first time Freddie bungled setting a fire."

"I still think we need to speak to Esme and Phillip together because I think they know more than they think they do," Jiff said. "The conversation Wallace will have with the police should get Phillip off the hook, assuming he will follow through and not disappear again."

"He won't disappear," I said, silently saying a prayer that I was right to have faith in him.

Chapter Fifteen

Monday a.m.

EARLY MONDAY MORNING while I was feeding Meaux and Isabella, and before having coffee, my cell phone rang. It was a very upset Jiff calling to tell me Phillip was checking his emails and saw where a fellow worker posted Ed was found in his fishing pirogue, dead from an apparent blow to the head. Phillip was told it appeared to be an accident since it was blunt force trauma to the head, as if he had slipped.

"Someone is cleaning house. Next is Phillip. Good thing Angie doesn't know where he is," Jiff said to me.

Jiff told me he was going to call the EPA legal office and advise them of what he had found on behalf of his clients, Ian Saucier and Phillip Wilson. With Ed Chauvin's death, he needed to move up meeting with them to show what Ed had sent him.

As I walked to my car to head to the office, Jiff asked me to call Phillip and Esme and see if they could meet us tonight after work. I said I'd set it up.

While I was thinking how close we were to coming to a conclusion and yet so far from proving it, my cell phone rang. It was Dante.

"Hey," I answered. "What's up?"

"First I want to tell you the Arson Investigator stated the fire was caused by gas left on in the house from the kitchen area. The Arson Investigator reported there was sufficient gas accumulated in the kitchen and throughout the first floor to suggest gas was left on for several hours. That's what caused the explosion. Know anything about that?" Dante asked.

"No, but I suspected as much since we heard the explosion from Jiff's boat, then saw the house on fire. The fireworks barge explosion followed a few seconds after that," I said.

"Before you ask, we only have the ID on the body in the house fire as Fred Finkelstein," Dante said. "There's not been any other DNA found on anyone else."

I didn't want to tell him I already suspected there would be no other DNA found. We had gotten past the point in every discussion where he told me to stay out of his ongoing investigation and I didn't want to mess that up. This was progress.

"Thanks for calling to tell me," I said.

"Seems Fred Finkelstein was a low life we've arrested many times for drugs. The good news is, it wasn't your friend in that fire, which makes me ask my next question: Where is Sophie Saucier, and for that matter, her husband, Ian Saucier?"

"Why do you think I know where they are?" I asked.

"Because you were there when it happened and every time you or your boyfriend show up at one of my cases that involve—witnesses, victims, perps—you know or you see something. So, where are they?"

"Have you made any arrests in this case yet? Like who might have tried to kill them?" I asked.

"*Tried to kill them...* See, that's what I mean," Dante said. "You know something. What is it?"

"I've been thinking that Angie Wilson, Phillip's wife, has had the most to gain from all of it. She gets the insurance money, the businesses, and she hated Sophie and Ian. If both are dead, she has her husband, their business and a lot of money."

"Not enough for an arrest," Dante said.

"Did you meet her? That alone should be enough for an arrest," I said.

"Maybe she and her husband are in cahoots," Dante said.

"Did you say 'cahoots'? Have you been watching old police sitcoms from the sixties? I think that's the last place I heard someone say 'cahoots'. Phillip is not in cahoots with the wife he wants to divorce. He should get a Gold Star or Medal of Honor for being married to her this long. He's a veteran you know, like you," I said.

"I know. I know a lot about all of them, just not where Sophie Saucier is," he said. "I'm almost satisfied—did you hear me—I said, almost satisfied, Ian Saucier was blown off that barge and the fishes made short work of whatever pieces they found."

"That's an unpleasant visual. Anyway, tomorrow I will bring you a witness that can put certain people in a certain place with a certain box of dynamite that ties all this together with a pretty bow on top," I said.

"Meet me now," he said.

"Can't. He's working," I said. "He can't lose his job. I'll bring him in first thing tomorrow."

"Tomorrow? Be at my office with your secret witness by nine o'clock," he said and hung up.

I made a quick call to the burner number and Wallace answered. I told him we would meet tomorrow instead of today. He said that was better for him because they asked him to work today and he would have tomorrow off. Wallace didn't have any problem meeting me early on Tuesday morning so I gave him the name of a coffee shop I knew to be close to the police station and said I'd buy him coffee and breakfast first. He agreed.

Next, I wrapped up some office work, made a few

client phone calls and set up appointments for later in the week, and then it would be time to hurry over to meet Frank while Julia was at her luncheon.

FRANK HAD SEVERAL swatches of fabric, lace, trims and a dozen sketches all spread out over the workspace on the enormous island in Julia's kitchen. He and Julia's housekeeper, Gloria, were looking at them when I walked in. Gloria was the sister of Woozie who had been my family's housekeeper since before I was born.

"Oh no, no, no," I said. "Gloria can't know about this," I said to Frank. I turned to Gloria and said, "You can't breathe a word of this. You absolutely can't tell Woozie. Did you tell Woozie already? Did you?" I collapsed onto a bar stool that was near the kitchen island. "No, Miz Brandy," Gloria said, "I don't see Woozie much anyways. Your secret safe cuz Woozie would want me dead if she thought I know you was getting married before she know," Gloria said taking her wig off and handing it to Frank where he stowed it in one of the kitchen cabinets. Gloria went about getting her bucket of cleaning supplies and a mop from a nearby closet.

"Gloria can keep a secret. She works here," Frank said pointing his finger straight up referring to Julia's office space on the second floor, "with the gestapo upstairs."

"We haven't told anyone so if anybody finds out, I'll know it's one of you two," I said hoping to instill fear into them since they had this knowledge. They were both unfazed. "We want to wait until we get everything ready before we announce."

"Cuz you don't want your mother meddling, I know," Gloria said and went about emptying the dishwasher.

"Or Julia," Frank said.

"Right," I said and then looked at the sketches Frank had spread out. There were at least ten of them. "Some of these are new since you first showed them to me."

"I did a couple more for you," he said proudly laying them out so I could see each one fully.

"Okay, now don't say which one you like out loud just yet," I said looking at them. "Gloria, you come over and choose which one you like and then we'll tell each other the one we each like best."

"I already knows which one I think you gonna look the best in," Gloria said.

"Me too," Frank chimed in.

I looked back and forth at them. "You already know which one you like best?"

"She's been watching me sketch here in the kitchen for weeks now. The kitchen is like no man's land to her highness," Frank said.

"Don't tell me until I'm ready," I said. "This might take a few minutes."

Choosing one was hard. Frank had some traditional long gowns, some ballet length dresses, and even a bridal suit that was very beautiful. He had made copies of each design and used colored pencils to fill in the drawings, each one in white, cream, and a soft pastel pink. I liked them all. By now, Frank was fidgeting, dying to tell me his favorite.

"This is a lot harder than I thought," I said. "But I think I know which one I like the best."

Frank had numbered all the sketches. He made Gloria stop emptying the dishwasher, and write down the number we each liked on a piece of paper and give it to him. He wrote his number down also. Then he turned them all over and we had all selected the same dress. I picked the cream version, Frank picked the pink pastel and Gloria picked white.

"This is good. You both think I'll look good in the dress I picked. This is really good. Thanks," I said hugging them both and tearing up. "Thank you both."

Frank went straight to his tape measure and began taking my measurements.

"Frank, we have a tentative date set for the first week in October," I said. "I have a meeting next week at the Aucoin House to see if they can make all the arrangements for that date. Is that enough time for you?"

"My lord, that's only eight or nine weeks away," he said grabbing his chest as if he was having a heart attack.

"Can you do it?" I asked with a wince on my face.

"Of course, I can. I just wanted to mess with you." He put his pencil behind his ear while he wrapped the tape around me and wrote down my measurements. "Besides, I want to take my time and make it perfect."

"It will be perfect," Gloria said. "You gonna be beautiful in that dress, baby."

Frank cut his own patterns and sewed almost everything by hand. I don't know how he did it, but he made outfits for Julia in record time. I knew he would make an extra effort for my wedding dress.

"This feels like it might move fast, Frank. We've looked at a house this past weekend and put in an offer," I said.

"A house? Wow, you deserve it. Do you need a manservant? I'd gladly give up the life here at the Hotel California. You call it Julia's guest house, but I'm the one who checked in and can never leave," Frank said.

"I'll come work for you if Woozie can't," Gloria said. "Frank be right about this hotel. They all crazy like the people out in California."

Frank just did one of his eye moves to let me know Gloria didn't get it.

"Frank, do you think you can make Woozie a dress for my wedding without her knowing?" I asked. "Don't you still have her measurements from the last dress you made for her?"

"Yes, I have them if she didn't get any bigger," Frank said brushing a hair from his pixie haircut away from his face like he was tossing long locks over his shoulder.

"She wore dat dress just last week to my niece's wedding," Gloria said as she resumed emptying the dishwasher.

"I'll pay for Woozie's dress. Gloria, please ask her what color she would like if she had another dress like that one in a way she doesn't suspect something is going on," I said.

"I already know," she answered me. "At the wedding she said that her peach dress was pretty, but her real color is rose, like a medium pink, not dark pink and not light pink. You can make her a medium pink dress and she will love it."

"All right," I said. "Frank, can this all be done by the first week in October?"

"It shall be, my Princess," he said winking at me. Frank looked at his watch. "Your wish is my command. We gotta wrap this up for today. Julia will be back from the luncheon soon. I'll call you for a fitting when I get it put together."

I hugged them both before leaving.

On the way back to the office I thought of a way I could validate what I wanted to tell Phillip and Esme if my assumption was right regarding Ian and Sophie. I would just have to pull up some records back at my office.

It took some time but I found what I was looking for. I had a message from Jiff's mom with some dates the manager at Aucoin House could meet with us. After checking my calendar, I called Mrs. Heinkel and gave her two dates that worked for me and asked is if that date worked for her, and she said yes. She told me she would call Christine and make the appointment for next Wednesday afternoon for us. I suggested I could pick her up and drive so we'd only have to park one car.

"Call this number," she said giving me a telephone number and an account number. "Our limo service will pick you up and bring you back to wherever you want. That's how I'm getting there."

Yes, being included in the Royal Family was starting to feel good.

Chapter Sixteen

Monday p.m.

THAT EVENING WE planned to meet with Phillip and Esme at Jiff's office. I got there before either of them. Felix brought Phillip in via the Bat Mobile and the Bat Cave secret entrance.

Jiff had some questions for Phillip while we waited for Esme.

"Phillip, if Ian parked at his boathouse where he met Freddie and got Freddie to give him a lift to the barge, then Ian's car should still be there, right?" I asked. "Do you have a set of keys for Ian's car?"

"No, I don't have keys but there might be a set at the office. Why do you ask?" Phillip asked.

"If Freddie rode with Ian, maybe Freddie took his car?" I asked.

"Freddie doesn't have a car. If he needs a car, he borrows Angie's. He has asked to borrow mine or the company van, but the answer was, and will always be, no," Phillip said. "I don't think Freddie has ever driven a vehicle sober."

"We know from Jack he didn't take his car when he left the marina," Jiff says. "I'll send Felix to the marina to look for Ian's car and see if Ian left his computer in it."

"Then Ian's car should still be at the boathouse and yes, Freddie should have stayed since Ian was his ride back after the fireworks," Phillip said. "Ian's car has not showed back up at the office if Freddie took it.

"We know he didn't stay because the party barge is at the boathouse," Jiff said. "And there is a witness that saw someone pick Freddie up on a motorcycle. He didn't take a car."

"Phillip, when did you get to the house fire?" I asked.

"Did you see Freddie at any time after he dropped Ian off at the barge? Angie? Did you see Angie at the house?" Jiff said.

"No, I didn't see Freddie, and Angie never showed up at Ian's house. I called her on the way there after I took the inventory to the riverfront. We were supposed to meet there and walk up on the levee with Sophie to watch the fireworks. I totally forgot with all the other events that were happening," Phillip said.

"Angie lost it when I called and said I was going on the fishing trip. She was agitated, more so than usual. When she answered, she immediately asked me if I had seen Freddie, so my guess is she hasn't seen him either. I told her I'd call him and ask him to watch the office for a few days, and she hurriedly told me never mind, she'd do it. She must know something. I hope Freddie didn't have anything to do with this."

"We need to ask you and Esme something. It would be better if you were both together when we do," I said.

"Let's wait for her," Jiff said. "She should be here any minute."

"What's this about?"

"Ian and Sophie, but let's wait until she gets here, Okay?" Jiff asked.

"Sure," he said.

After everyone was together, I told Esme and Phillip the three DNA hits were two cremated remains, most likely Ian's parents in urns on the mantle, with the third DNA identified a male.

"Have the police identified the male?" Esme asked, her voice cracked when she did.

"It's not Ian," Jiff added quickly. He looked at Phillip and said, "It's Angie's brother, Freddie."

Phillip sat looking down at his hands, saying, "Oh God, I'm so sorry."

"We need to ask you both if you remember anything else about the day of or days before the 4th when all this happened," Jiff said. "Brandy thinks Ian and

Sophie are alive."

"If I knew or thought they were alive I'd tell you," Esme quickly answered.

"Me too," Phillip said.

"Oh, no, I believe you both think they are dead. We did too," I said. "I started to question some things you told us when they felt off, or not right."

"That's what Brandy is good at," Jiff said.

"You don't think they faked their own deaths, do you?" Phillip asked.

"No, I think they both narrowly escaped the plan to kill them, and then Ian, being smart, figured they would be the prime suspects in each other's murder along with the insurance money that is out there to claim," Jiff said.

"I've known a few days that the DNA at the house was male and I was afraid you might think it was Ian so I didn't want to say anything until we were certain. I'm pretty sure the police thought it was Ian, too, although no one told me that. Basically, there were no bodies or DNA evidence to prove Ian or Sophie were at either location when it happened," I said. "No bodies, no forensic evidence, no deaths."

I asked Esme about Blast and why Sophie left him with her. "Something you told me the first time we met has been gnawing at me, what was it? Oh right, you said Sophie usually kept Blast in her master bedroom with classic music playing so he wouldn't be scared or hear the party downstairs, right?"

Esme said, "Yes. And there's something else I just remembered. Sophie told me Angie was there that morning when the deliveries were being made for the party. I remember her saying Angie had stopped by to see if she could help her with anything...Angie help Sophie? That should have been a red flag." She looked at Phillip, "I'm sorry Phillip, but we know how Angie felt about Sophie."

Phillip nodded and looked at his hands.

"I should have seen that, or told you. I've been so overwrought with losing Sophie and Ian, waiting to hear where or if they are found. That piece of info just didn't seem all that important then, but it does now," Esme said.

Jiff and I looked at each other. Angie was at Ian and Sophie's house the morning of the fire.

"Anything else about the day of the fire?" I asked.

"Sophie said Angie left with her at the same time, Sophie left home to bring Blast to my house," Esme said tears rolling down her face. "She was going to kill Sophie, wasn't she?"

"Well, it would explain how the gas was left on," I said.

"I think she left the gas on for when Sophie returned home for an explosion to happen. Anything, like turning on a light switch can set it off. There were motorcycle tire tracks cut deep in the back lawn of the house. I think it was Freddie's bike, but where is the bike now?" Jiff asked. "We know Freddie was picked up by someone on a motorcycle from Ian's boathouse. I'm sure he got to Ian's house on it and since no one saw them come or go—there was no neighborhood crime footage—I think they rode in over the levee."

Phillip tells them Freddie always rode a motorcycle. "He had an old Harley he was using while one of his biker buddies did his time in Angola. He still has some old buddies in that club, but they won't let Freddie hang or ride with them anymore."

"Club? You mean gang," Jiff said.

I turned to face Jiff and said, "They prefer to be called a club, a motorcycle club. Don't you want to be politically correct?" Then I turned back to Esme and Phillip, "Two other things. One is Jiff's investigator found out that Angie's dad, uncle, and brother were getting payments from the labs that you and Ian used to send your samples to. She also found where Freddie recently bought a brand new motorcycle he registered in his name. There's no record of financing it so he must have paid cash for a new Harley about two weeks ago."

"What's the other?" Esme asked.

"The other is the homeless man that was in your

Richards Building. Phillip, remember when we asked you about the dynamite he saw there?" Jiff asked.

"Yes," Phillip said.

"Well, there was a homeless man camped out at that building and the graffiti cleaner called your office and someone who answered, claiming to be the owner, called the police to have him removed," Jiff said.

"That would most likely be Angie," Phillip said. "Or she made Freddie do it."

Jiff and I nodded in agreement.

"I found him—the homeless man," I said. "He's an old biker brother of Freddie's, but he can put Freddie, Angie and her uncle, plus another man he didn't recognize, at your building removing the dynamite on July 3rd, the day before the explosion."

Esme and Phillip were sitting with shocked looks on their faces when Felix returned to the office.

I added, "The homeless man's name is Wallace. He is going with me tomorrow to the police to tell them what he saw."

"We think Angie's brother had an old club friend pick him up and ride him out to the house to watch it burn," I said. "Wallace said Freddie was a classic arsonist. When the house hadn't exploded, we think Freddie went in to see why or to light a match. When he opened the door and turned on the light it probably sparked and exploded the gas. Freddie's friend rode off on Freddie's new motorcycle the way they came in, over the levee. If the police can find him, he could verify he took Freddie there."

Jiff added, "Jack, someone I know who lives on his yacht, told us he saw Freddie leave the boathouse and was picked up by someone on a motorcycle. There were motorcycle tracks at Sophie's house and a male dead body we now know is Freddie."

Phillip said, "There is something else I remembered while at your condo, Jiff."

All eyes turned to Phillip.

"There's a petty cash box in the safe, and we usually keep about $5K in it for emergencies. I went to pull out some cash to tip a courier and noticed it was gone. Ian took it and left a note saying, *P, don't worry, I borrowed it and plan to put it back, Ian.* He didn't date it so I'm not sure exactly when he took it."

"When did you last see the money, that you're sure of?" Jiff asked.

"Maybe a week before the explosion on the 4th."

"If Ian planned to take it, wouldn't he have told you? That's a lot of money," I asked.

"He did tell me, just in the note, so now I'm thinking it had to be after the explosion. He and I, maybe Sophie, are the only ones who have the combination to that safe. Angie doesn't know it although she has asked about it many times. Ian left the note, and it was in his handwriting. I just don't know when that was. I forgot about it since I only use it if we have casual workers to pay or for a Cash Only Delivery or COD. But that was a lot of money, and I know Ian would have told me why he was taking it or needing it, even if it was personal. We talked about everything."

"Ian always worried that if we had another city-wide evacuation and needed gas money to leave town, then we'd have a stash. Remember, in Katrina, nobody's phones worked or local banks to get money until you got way out of town. There was still about $500 in there so I didn't think much of it at the time."

"Right," I said. Jiff nodded in agreement.

"He left five hundred dollars in there. He didn't take it all," Phillip said. "Anytime we left the number or said the number 500, it was our code to be careful, or that one of us was in trouble. That's what we used in the military. We haven't used it since we were in the service. So, now I realize Ian was leaving me a message. He's in trouble and maybe he was telling me I was too."

Felix returned about forty minutes later with Ian's laptop. Felix was quite handy to have around. He obviously knew how to get into cars, even without keys.

Once I had the laptop, Jiff found Ian's letter with the passwords and we logged in. I found a list of all the lab files with the original results and then Ian's notes on what he and Phillip discovered when they tested their identical samples. This would be the nail in the coffin for Angie and pals when Jiff gives it to the DA and the EPA attorneys along with the financial records Michelle researched.

"We still don't know where Ian and Sophie are," Esme said.

"I do," I said. "You said Sophie brought Blast to your house because your parents have a vet clinic, but were going to be in Europe for three weeks. You said they gave their staff a three-week vacation, right? I searched and found the name of the vet clinic your parents own. I did a search on any commercial phone records billed to the clinic, and there's been calls made from that clinic since the 4th of July. I only have access to business phone records."

"No one's supposed to be there. My parents gave everyone three weeks off at the same time and blacked out those dates. They don't even board anyone's pets during that three weeks. They do that every year," Esme said.

"Do you have keys to their home and clinic?" Jiff asked.

"We all have keys. You think they are staying there," Esme said. "Of course, they have everything they need at my parents' home or at the clinic, computer, clothes, food, money, car…everything."

"Anyone up for a drive?" Jiff asked.

We all left through the Bat Cave exit. Felix drove us in the company limo parked down in the secret parking section. Another new, fun fact about Jiff's firm I learned. They have a limo.

Esme gave Felix the address of her parents' home out in Eden Isles. Their vet clinic was on the main road into their subdivision with access to their residence via a connecting path across a footbridge over a canal. We rode in silence for almost thirty minutes out to the home.

Both Ian and Sophie answered the door. The surprised look on their faces turned into a happy, but tearful reunion with Esme and Phillip. After some hugs and handshakes all around, we were all invited inside.

After an informal introduction as to who I was, we all went to the living room where Ian and Sophie told us their side of what happened on the night of both events.

"Hope you all don't hate us," Sophie said.

"I feel like you both should hate me for bringing Angie into our lives," Phillip said.

Ian said, "I wasn't sure who was going to hurt us, but I knew one of Angie's relatives were or were going to have someone do it after I saw the dynamite. I only had time to phone Sophie, set the timer and jump off the barge to swim to shore. The weather and the current were bad and it took me a while to make it to the seawall."

He had spotted the dynamite in the bottom of the fireworks display Freddie had packed for the 4th as they loaded his van with the crates to take to the barge. As soon as Freddie left him, Ian called Sophie and made a plan on the fly.

Sophie said, "Ian called me when Angie was there. He told me to get away from her and take Blast out of the house. 'Don't tell her where you're going. Mislead her. Leave her there or tell her you'll be right back. Just get away from her,'" he said.

Ian put his arm around her on the sofa as she tilted her head toward his shoulder.

"We are just so grateful to be alive and not hurt," Sophie said. "We've wanted to call and tell you, but Ian was afraid the police would blame us."

"And with those life insurance policies, I felt we'd be the only suspects and the police would close the case on it with us in jail."

Ian and Sophie told their side of the story through tearful renderings. It was so last minute to try to find a place to board Blast, Sophie decided to just take Blast to Esme. Sophie told Esme, Angie was around all morning annoying her and asking what she could do to help, but then didn't do anything Sophie asked her to. She said, "I didn't realize why she was there until Ian called and I got so scared."

No one except Esme admitted to seeing Sophie that Thursday morning. Esme said Sophie told her she walked out with Angie under the pretense of taking Blast to board.

Jiff said, "Angie lied. Now we know she was at your home."

According to the credit card charges, trays of burgers and all the fixings were delivered from Whole Foods. Sophie said any one of the delivery people could testify Angie was there.

Ian said he told Sophie to meet him at the place they had their first date in high school. That was at the picnic shelter on Lakeshore Drive next to the Mardi Gras Fountain. He told her not to answer her phone for anyone, and as soon as she reached the meeting point to throw her phone in the lake. He said he'd be there, but he wouldn't have his phone after he hung up with her.

Sophie parked her car near her home, maybe three blocks away so none of the neighbors would see her. She put on the sunhat she kept in the car and walked a couple of miles to a coffee shop where she had an Uber pick her up and drop her at a coffee shop close to her parents' house. She took the clinic vehicle and drove to the picnic shelter along the Lakefront to wait for Ian. He set a timer to start the fireworks and then jumped off and swam to shore. Rather than fight the current, he let it take him where it dumped him out near the University of New Orleans close to the Lakefront airport. He walked along the lake side of the levee until he reached the seawall. Then he walked about six steps down, out of view from the road or anyone driving by until he reached the shelter where he told Sophie to pick him up. Once they were together, Sophie handed him her phone and Ian threw it into the lake. Then, they took a chance and drove to the office that night to get the cash out of the safe while everyone was at the fire.

After Ian got the cash, they went to hide out at her parents' house until Jiff or the police figured it out. They were terrified if they came forward, another attempt would be made on one or both of them or they would be arrested by the police.

Chapter Seventeen

Tuesday a.m.

WALLACE AGREED TO meet me at the coffee shop near NOPD on Broad Street at 9:00 a.m. I was nervous someone would arrest him for something before he got a chance to meet Dante and Detective Taylor. He was waiting out front when Jiff and I arrived. He walked in wearing a nice pair of dark pants, a white shirt, short sleeves, and a tie. He held his helmet under his arm and he had had a haircut and shave.

"You look very nice, Wallace. Thank you for coming," I said.

"I got these clothes at the thrift store called Bloomingdeals," he said. "I had a job there yesterday, and they let me pick whatever I need for today in addition to paying me. I thought that was super nice."

"That was nice," I said.

"Can we just go there now?" Wallace asked. "I'm kinda nervous and want to get this over with."

"Sure. It's close so we can walk," Jiff said.

After we made it through the metal detectors and security, I asked, "Where's Mr. Nutty?"

"Who?" Wallace asked.

"Your baby squirrel," I said. "I gave him a name...Mr. Nutty."

Smiling, Wallace said, "That fits him. He's in my helmet." Wallace tilted his helmet to show the tiny creature asleep under the bandana I had seen him wear on his head. He had passed it to the security guard and it had not gone through x-ray. I figured Dante and Taylor would never speak to me again if that baby squirrel jumps out of the helmet and runs up Wallace's arm to sit on his head.

"I'll hold your helmet while you go in and talk to the detectives," I said. "Jiff will go in with you as your attorney so the police don't get any ideas. I know these two, and they will have to deal with me if they try to pull a fast one."

Wallace reached into one of his pockets and gave me a handful of peanuts he already shelled. He nodded toward Mr. Nutty.

I smiled and took the peanuts.

Jiff extended his hand to shake Wallace's. "Thanks for coming and doing this. You being here is important to some great friends of mine. She's right. The two detectives you are gonna talk to are afraid of her," he said, nodding in my direction.

I made my tsk sound and waved my hand away to dismiss what Jiff said while holding on to the helmet. The three of us went to join the others sitting on a bench waiting for their interviews. I introduced Wallace to Ian, Sophie, Esme and Phillip.

Wallace was called in first and Jiff went with him. Later, Jiff gave me every detail of Wallace's statement. Wallace told them who he saw at the Richards Street building, on what date and what they were doing. He named them and verified it in a photo lineup. He maintained he didn't know who the third guy was, but he did describe him and gave a good description of a tattoo the man had on his upper right arm.

After Wallace's statement, Jiff sat with each of the others while they gave their statements to Detective Taylor and Captain Deedler. Deedler dispatched Hanky to the marina to get Jack Dahl's statement on seeing Freddie on the night of the 4th.

While we were waiting for Sophie to finish with Detective Taylor, we were brought into a conference room to wait. I said I'd go look for coffee. That's when I saw three uniformed policemen bring in Angie Wilson with two men I assumed to be her father and her uncle. They escorted each one of the three into a separate interrogation room. She didn't see me.

Dante came out and said he would be interviewing

Angie Wilson. I thought about telling him to bring his stun gun. I decided to let him find out on his own.

It didn't take long for Angie to rat out the others. Dante came out and thanked us all for coming in. He said he had to finish interviews with the suspects, but it was all looking good. He felt they had enough evidence and testimony to go to the District Attorney's office.

Jiff later learned that Angie, thinking Ian and Sophie were dead, gave a statement to the police saying Phillip planned the whole thing, to kill Ian, divorce her and run off with Sophie. Unfortunately, she heard there was a tragic accident that killed Sophie in a fire. Police questioned Angie and caught her in several lies. She says she saw Phillip packing the dynamite in the bottom of the firework boxes on the day Ian and Phillip were supposed to set off for the big display. Angie denied going to their house that morning and seeing Sophie. When the police told her they had a witness that put her there, she blamed it on her brother who went there to see it explode. He was the arsonist. Then in a panic, Angie claimed she left with Sophie to take her stupid dog to a groomer. The police informed Angie the Arson Investigator said the gas had been on since around the time they both left, which made her the prime suspect. Since there was a body found in the fire, she would be charged with homicide during the commission of a felony.

She flipped on her brother, Freddie, saying he was the one who suggested she turn on the gas. She had not been told he was the body found in the fire. Thinking she'd get a deal for immunity, she told the police everything about the labs, payoffs and who killed Ed Chauvin, saying her husband, Phillip, planned the entire crime. She never asked for an attorney. She offered to be a witness for the prosecution until she was arrested. Then she wanted a deal to testify against the others after she just made statements implicating them. Like I said, dumb as a rock.

Police put out an APB out on Freddie's motorcycle, and it was found in less than six hours, along with the third man who helped Freddie and Angie's father move the dynamite. To avoid being charged with homicide, Freddie's helper confessed. He identified Angie, her dad, and Freddie as the ones who took him to where the dynamite was, helped move it, and pack it with fireworks. He said they discussed everything they planned to do with it and named names, locations, times, and places. The police didn't need Angie as a witness.

Just then, Dante walked up with Detective Taylor and offered a half-hearted attempt at thanking me and Jiff for finding Wallace and getting him to come forward as a witness. He also mentioned it was good we found Ian and Sophie alive.

"It was all her," Jiff said shaking Dante's hand and Taylor's. "Brandy knows everybody in this city." He checked his watch and said, "We're off to see a man about a house."

Dante and Taylor's heads whipped around to look at me. I just smiled my goofy grin that takes over my face whenever I get nervous. I turned and walked out with Jiff.

I barely heard Taylor say, "Captain, you should hire her."

Chapter Eighteen

Two weeks later

TWO WEEKS HAD passed since the day at the precinct and most things were back to normal or as close as it gets in New Orleans. Our offer on the Prytania Street Victorian house was accepted, and my fear of home ownership gave way to excitement. I always thought fear and excitement were on either side of the same coin. Jiff and I made plans to close on our new home in six weeks, right before our wedding. It was going to be a hectic few weeks until our big day, but we were both so excited.

So far I had avoided telling my parents or having the sit down with Dante regarding it, but I knew it was coming. I planned to tell Dante first. Frank was keeping our secret under wraps so there wasn't a big chance of Julia broadcasting my news before I decided to announce it.

Esme called while we were on the way home after the inspections on our new house and said she was inviting everyone to her home for a dinner party tonight. She said to bring our Schnauzers! Our two could meet Blast and Sparkler. She told all of us she had a surprise she wanted to share and to bring our appetites.

When we arrived with Schnauzers and a bottle of Dom Perignon in hand, Esme greeted us at the door with hugs and kisses. We were old friends by now. Everyone was already there, and it was a bark fest for the first five minutes. Esme motioned all of us to the side door she opened into the big side garden, so Blast and Sparkler could run outside with Meaux and Isabella in hot pursuit. While she served drinks, we all sat outside to watch as they played hard, chasing each other around the garden.

Jiff asked if she would pour the champagne for everyone. When she came out with six flutes of the bubbly, Jiff made a toast. As everyone raised their glasses, he said, "Here's to finding Ian and Sophie alive, avoiding Phillip's arrest and to the house Brandy and I have decided to buy together. May our darkest days be behind us!"

Ian hugged Sophie and said, "To your new home. That sounds promising."

"Here, here!" voices chimed as the glasses clinked.

Ian toasted to all of us for being true friends and not giving up on him and Sophie.

There was plenty of comradery to go around with Jiff, Ian, and Phillip seeing each other socially again since law school. They had lots to catch up on while Esme or Sophie confirmed or called into question some of their escapades they told that grew larger over the years.

I noticed Esme and Phillip were never more than an arm's length from each other. If either one went inside to retrieve another bottle of wine, the other one followed under the pretense of helping and they came back and stood next to each other again.

As the sun started to set, and the dogs were all lying at our feet panting, Esme called for a move indoors, nodding at the dogs. She said, "I think they are ready to go back inside. I'll check on dinner."

When she opened the door, the four ran in and flopped on the cool hardwood floors with all feet spread out like frogs, panting, and smiling. I can always tell when Meaux is smiling after a fun outing.

Jiff started to say as he looked at Isabella sprawled out, "Ours are rude…"

"I beg your pardon?" I asked with mock indignation.

"Beg. You said the key word. Ours beg at the table, so if you have a baby gate, we could put them in the kitchen or laundry room," Jiff said.

"Are you kidding?" Esme said coming out of the

kitchen with another bottle of champagne. It seems we weren't the only ones who planned to celebrate. She nodded toward her dog and Ian's, "Sparkler and Blast wrote the book on begging. Your two seem to be in good, or shall I say, bad company?"

"Blast must have learned that bad habit since he's been here," Ian teased taking two glasses and handing one to Sophie.

"Uhhh, Blast taught Sparkler," Esme said. "My dog was, correction…is… perfect."

"To Schnauzers…the perfect dogs," Jiff toasted.

"Here, here," Ian said as we all clinked our glasses in a toast.

We sat down to eat, and Wallace came out of the kitchen bringing bowls of gumbo on a platter to set down in front of us.

"Wallace! This must be Esme's surprise," Jiff said.

"I heard Phillip and Ian discussing hiring him to cook at the new building when their lab is ready and to run errands when needed," Esme said. "I just decided to put him to work immediately until Phillip and Ian are ready for him…as a thank you for stepping forward in the investigation."

"I have a job with Phillip and Ian's new lab. Right now, I'm cooking dinners for them. I hope you like it," he said and looked a little nervous in the chef's white jacket I'm sure Esme bought for him to wear.

"That jacket suits you, Chef," I said. "Whatever you're cooking in the kitchen smells divine."

Esme said smiling and reaching for Phillip's hand, "This dinner is compliments of Phillip and I to say thank you to Jiff and Brandy for your help, on behalf of all of us."

"You are most welcome," Jiff said for us.

Phillip asked, "Is everyone ready to eat?"

Meaux barked a yes as we all laughed and lifted our soup spoons.

THE END

Dear reader,

Thank you so much for reading my books. I hope you enjoyed them. Since reviews are very important to Indie authors, if you did enjoy this I would be delighted if you would be so kind as to leave a review.

I always want to hear from and connect with my readers. Please feel free to contact me at any time with questions, ideas for new books, or just plain anything. I am happy to answer any questions. Visit my website to see more of my books and join my newsletter at www.colleenmooney.com.

Once again, many thanks for reading my book!

Colleen